Fallin' For a Boss 3

By: Lucinda John

A letter to my readers

Hey y'all!! I am happy to present you guys with my fifth book with Shan Presents. The love that you guys have been showing me has been unbelievable. The amount of love that I receive from you guys on Facebook warms my heart. All I ever wanted to do was to write. I had a lot of people tell me that there was no career in writing and not to quit my day job, but there is a God and what God wrote can't no man erase. I believe that I have finally found my purpose; writing has really become a big part of my life. This is really my passion and a dream come true. I would really like to thank all of you for your support. If it wasn't for you and your support I wouldn't have been able to present you guys with my fifth book. I must have re-written this book three times trying it to get it right just for y'all. I hope that you guys enjoy it. This book is dedicated to you!! Happy reading and don't forget to leave a review.

Love,

Lucinda John

Please text SHAN to 22828 to stay up to date with new releases, sneak peeks, contests, and more…

Previously…

Lala

"Lala, hurry up or we're going to be late!" Stacks
yelled.

I was in the room looking for my pearl set that would
go perfectly with the all-white Vera Wang dress I was
wearing. I didn't know where we were off to in such a
rush. Earlier today, Stacks sent a make-up artist, hair
stylist, and a nail tech, and had them pamper me. He then
came home with this all white dress and some white flats
and asked me to hurry up and get dressed.

"Why don't you have on the flats I bought you?" he
frowned.

"You can't wear flats with this dress, that's tacky."

"Well, I sure as hell don't want you walking around
in heels eight months pregnant."

"These are not heels, they're wedges. Similar to flats,
but a little higher," I smiled

"You're dressed, so what's taking you so long?"

"I can't find my pearls, how am I supposed to accessorize?"

"If you would have just hurried up and went with the flow, you would have seen that I had you covered."

He pulled out a red velvet box from behind his back and opened it. I started to drool over the beautiful diamonds that shined so brightly. He clasped the necklace around my neck while placing soft kisses on me.

"Mmmm," I moaned.

I was ready to take off my dress and fuck him on the spot. Since I entered my third trimester, my sex drive was on an all-time high. If he sneezed, I would get hot, wet, and ready to fuck.

"A quickie before we go, please?" I begged.

Raising my dress a little, he pulled out his dick. He held me up against the wall and fucked me real rough. I screamed out in pleasure as he bit down hard on my neck. Thrusting in and out of me with nice long strokes, he was driving my ass crazy. My eyes rolled to the back of my head as I squeezed my pussy muscles around his dick, sucking his dick dry before feeling a gush of fluids.

"You sure your water ain't break?" Stacks joked.

"Naw, you ain't stroking like that," I laughed.

He laid me on the bed and came back with rags to clean us up.

Adjusting my dress and touching up my make-up, I made sure my hair was still in place before we left. When we got to a red light, Stacks handed me a blindfold to put over my eyes. Making sure it was secure and blocked my vision, he made his way to our destination.

The car slowed down, and then came to a complete stop. I heard him open and close his door then come around to open mine.

"You better not fall or I'm kicking your ass for wearing them damn heels," he fussed and guided me to wherever we were headed to.

Removing the blindfold, the whole room screamed out surprise at the top of their lungs. The ballroom was decorated in soft pink and white, with banners saying, "It's A Girl."

I remembered Stacks asking me what I wanted to do for a baby shower, and I told him I really didn't want one.

"I'm going to get you," I said and punched him in the arm before I planted a soft kiss on his lips.

Lisa came over a placed a 'Mommy to be' sash around my body and a tiara on my head.

"I'ma get you, too! Why didn't you tell me?" I asked.

"Stacks threatened to kill me and I love my life."

"How are you holding up?"

"I'm good. Why you ask?"

I nodded my head towards Ralph and Kandi. They'd been really kicking it. He tried to bring her to my house one time, and I shut that shit down quick. I made him take her ass back to where she came from. Lisa was the only friend I needed. I ain't want no random bitch around me.

"Girl bye! I'm not on that," she lied.

"Girl you can fool every motherfucker in here, but you can't fool me."

"Today is your day let's discuss this later."

Making my way to my table, it was decorated really nice. Two large containers filled with money were at the end of each of the tables. As the guest filled the containers with money, the security guards took them to the back to empty them. Everyone was enjoying themselves, eating, drinking, dancing, and stopping to play the baby shower games. Glancing at the gift table, I thought I was going to pass out. They had to rope off the whole back area just so there was room for the large load of gifts.

"Can I have this dance?" Stacks asked.

"Yes, you can."

Michael Jackson's slow version of 'Love Never Felt So Good', was playing as we swayed to the beat.

"You know I love you right?" I said.

"Yes, I do and I love you more."

He leaned down and slipped his tongue in my mouth.

"When are you going to be my wife?"

"I don't have my ring."

He slipped the ring back on my finger. I examined it because it looked different.

"Did you get me a new ring?"

"No, I improved it, just like I improved myself. The ring symbolizes the changes I've made to become fully committed to you."

At that moment, I knew God had sent him down especially for me. He was everything I wanted in a man and more. Yes, we had our moments, but our relationship had lasted throughout all of the things we had been through. Watching our friends and family celebrate the arrival of our baby girl brought tears in my eyes. This is what I prayed for when I used to lay in bed crying because James never made it home.

God was answering my prayers all at once, and I felt my blessings overflowing.

The baby shower started to wind down as the waiters began to clean up. Stacks had to order a mini U-Haul truck just to carry the baby's belongings home. After saying our goodbyes and thanking everyone for coming, we made our way home.

"What's up with Ralph and Kandi?" I asked Stacks.

"None of your business, so stay out of it."

"I just wanted to know if he was really feeling her."

"He's coping. He really does love Lisa, but with men it's an ego thing. Things will fall in place. Like I said, stay out of it."

When we finally got home, Stacks stayed downstairs showing the men where to put the baby's things. I went to the master bathroom and ran some warm water. My feet were really killing me. Immersing in the warm water, I threw my head back and allowed the jets in the tub to massage my body. I felt a sharp pain shoot down my back to my vagina, but I ignored it. Another sharp pain hit me again, so I decided to get out of the tub.

As soon as my feet touched the floor, another pain ran through my body leaving me doubled over in excruciating agony. Trying to stand all the way up, a gush of liquid came out of me.

"STACCCCCCCCCCCKS!!!!!!!!!!" I yelled.

I heard him running up the stairs.

"Baby you good?"

"No, we have to get to the hospital, my water broke."

Running to the room, he grabbed me something to wear. After dressing me, he helped me get in the car before he went back inside to get my bags.

"Oh, God, it hurts!" I yelled.

"Baby, remember to breathe, you have to breathe."

"Fuck breathing, I want her out of me. NOW!"

Stacks floored it as we headed to the hospital. Once we stopped at a red light, he pulled out his phone and called Lisa, and then Ralph telling them to meet us at the hospital.

Before another contraction hit me, the car was raided with bullets. Stacks was trying to drive away from them as fast as possible, and we ended up crashing into a tree, and landing in a ditch.

"Lala, are you okay?" he asked.

"The head, I feel the pressure of the baby's head!" I cried.

"Okay, I want you to relax for me and then push."

"I can't do it, Stack. It hurts so badly."

"C'mon, Lala, push, please?"

I held onto Stacks' hand and started pushing with all my might. I noticed he was no longer saying anything. Looking over at him, I could see he was a bloody mess, and his eyes were closed as he laid his head against the window.

"Stacks, baby wake!" I panicked.

"I'm here, baby I'm not going nowhere," he said. His voice was fading in and out.

After pushing our little girl out, I used some eyebrow scissors to cut the umbilical cord. Wrapping her in my bloody robe, I put her in Stacks' lap as I felt another pain shoot through my body. Preparing to push out the afterbirth, I started to push with everything in me. I felt something drop and then more crying. Looking down, it was another baby.

"Oh, God, Stacks it's another baby."

"Another baby?" he weakly asked.

"Yes, we have twins!"

He tried to smile, but started violently coughing up blood.

"My miracles," he said trying to reach of our son.

"Thank you, Lala, for giving me my kids. Let them know that daddy loves them. I love you, too." He leaned his head back again, but this time he didn't budge as I tried to shake him.

"Stacks, baby wake up please! I can't do this without you, please!" I cried right along with my kids.

Someone started breaking down the door. They grabbed me out of the car, and then the babies, followed by Stacks.

"Ma'am, are you hurt?" the paramedic asked.

"Save him, please save him." I cried as my body began to tremble.

Watching his lifeless body on the pavement, I felt my knees get weak. I instantly became dizzy. The world started spinning as Stacks' final words to me replayed in my head. I couldn't believe this was happening to me. Hours ago, we were so happy. It wasn't supposed to end like this!

I heard my babies crying in the far distance. I still wasn't able to wrap my head around the fact that I'd just given birth to twins.

Watching the paramedics do all they could to resuscitate Stacks to no avail made my heart heavy. My stomach started to turn as I released all the food I ate today before collapsing on his body.

Chapter 1

Lala

Six Months Later…

The sound of my Gucci red bottoms echoed through the building with every step I took. Walking inside of the conference room, I took my place at the head of the table. Ralph sat to my right and Carla was to my left, the other workers were sitting around the table waiting for me to speak. Every time I took a seat in this brown, Italian leather chair, my mind instantly reverted to Stacks. It had been six long months without him and I still had wounds that weren't completely healed. Losing my soul mate pained me deeply and with every passing day, I was slowly teaching myself how to cope. Pushing Stacks out of my mind, I cleared my throat and began to speak.

"This month we're doubling up, if you think your team can't handle that amount of weight, let me know, so

I can go out and recruit niggas that can." I sat back and watched the facial expression of all the men before continuing "Ralph is going to handle all of the drops and pick ups, if you have any question or concerns report to him."

Looking over at Carla, I noticed that she seemed uninterested in what I had to say. Every since I stepped in and took Stacks' place she'd been acting real salty towards me. I didn't know what her problem was, but she had better put that petty shit aside. Looking over the reports, her team was slacking. Ralph was bringing in over one hundred grand, and Carla only had a measly forty grand to show for everything. What pissed me off was that she was re-upping and getting more dope than Ralph.

"If the money ain't adding up at the end of the month, there will be problems. Partners or not, I expect my two lieutenants to make goal." I intensely stared in Carla's eyes so that she could know that it was mainly directed to her.

"Good job like always, Ralph, you always deliver," I smirked while making her feel shitty in front of her men. "Ralph, I want you to take over the West and East side; those two areas are where the most money is made and I can't afford to have this bitch fuck shit up," I said adding salt to Carla's wounds.

"Excuse me?" she asked.

"You're excused!"

"How are you going to take my territory from me?"

"Easy. I'm the head bitch in charge. What I say goes."

"Wait until Papa hears about this."

"Tell your Papa, do I look like I give a fuck?" I snapped.

"You'll regret this."

"Is that a threat?" I asked with a raised brow.

"Take it how you want it. Let's go fellas," she said gathering her men before leaving. I knew I would never hear the end of it once Stacks' father got wind of what just gone down. But I didn't really care because she was causing us to lose too much money.

"You're free to dismiss yourselves," I said and cleared the room out, and then took a seat.

"Sis, you ok?" Ralph asked

I looked up at him with a face filled with tears. I was beyond hurt; I was lost, confused, and scared.

"It's gon' be straight sis don't even stress it," Ralph tried to assure me, but deep down inside I knew better. The only thing that could make things better was having Stacks here next to me.

"Let me take you to lunch."

"No, I'm fine. I have to stop by the clinics," I said pulling out my iPad and thumbing through my schedule for today. I owned three women's clinics to make the illegal money I was making legit. I was living out my dream while maintaining Stacks' pharmaceutical business, as well. Initially, Ralph was supposed to take over since Stacks passed, but Stacks' father wanted to keep everything in the family, so he groomed me to take over.

Walking to the bathroom, I washed my face and re applied my make-up. Having the twins did my body really well as I admired my full figure in the mirror. The ten pounds that I couldn't get rid of looked really good on me. Instead of trying to lose it, I just went to the gym three times a week to make sure my body was nice and toned.

Straitening out my Donna Karen pants suit, I grabbed my matching Gucci bag and made my way to the all white Chrysler convertible I recently purchased. Money was flowing like water for me. I had enough money to fix this fucked up economy.

"Hey, Shelly, how is everything?" I asked one of my head nurses as I walked behind the nurses' station.

"Everything is going well. Dani called out again, so I'm stuck doing her work," she sighed and handed me a stack of paperwork. "Here are the orders that need to be put in."

"I am going to have a talk with her," I said and took the folder before heading to my office. I made me a cup of coffee using the Keurig Elite brewing system that I had in my office. Making sure my coffee was light and sweet, I took a seat at my desk and powered on my Apple MacBook Pro. Tears instantly flooded my eyes as the picture of Stacks and I popped up on the screen. I stared at the picture while my mind wondered back to that horrific day that changed my life.

"Ma'am, we have to take him," the paramedic said and tried to pull me off of him as soon as I gained consciousness.

"No!" I yelled "Stacks, baby come back to my please!" I cried and kissed his lips. As I was kissing him, I felt him struggling to breath.

"He's awake, help him! Help him now!" I screamed like a mad woman as I snatched the paramedic by the collar. The police officer came over and tried to restrain me. Punching him in the face, I demanded that he let me go so that I could be by Stacks' side.

"Ma'am, if you don't calm down, I will be forced to arrest you. Under the circumstances, I would hate to have to arrest you," the fat donut eating pig said

"Fuck you," I spat as I still tried to wiggle away
"Help him!" I yelled

I watched as the paramedic loaded him inside of the ambulance and drove away. I wanted to cry out tears of joy because I had hope that my man was going to be ok. The paramedic then helped me inside of the bus, so that I could go to the hospital and receive medical assistance.

After the doctors ran tests on me and the babies, they informed me that everything was ok and allowed me to bond with them. Stacks' words 'My miracles' played in my head as I gave them their names; Amire and Amiracle.

Amire looked as if his father spit him out, however, Amiracle looked like a mini me. I was going crazy waiting for Ralph to come back with an update of Stacks' condition. His injuries were critical, so they had to bring him to the University of Miami Hospital. Every time the phone would ring, my heart would stop and I would pray that it was Ralph with good news.

I was breastfeeding Amire, when Ralph finally decided to show up. I could see the stressed look on his face and my heart began to beat out of my chest. I burped the baby and laid him down in the bassinet next to Amiracle and braced myself for what I was about to hear. Ralph had his head in his hands and when I heard him sniffle, it confirmed my worst nightmare.

"How is he?" I asked, I had to hear him say it.

He looked up at me with his blood shot, red eyes as the tears continue to pour out of them.

"Is he going to be ok?"

"Lala he...."

"HE WHAT?!"

"He didn't make it."

"How??!!!" I yelled and tried to swallow the big lump that had now formed in my throat. "He was breathing." I began to hysterically cry.

"The ambulance caught on fire on the way to the hospital."

"What?"

"The ambulance, it went up in flames, by the time I was able to make it down that street, it was up in flames."

"But I don't get it."

"A male body was confirmed being found."

"This is too much." *I began to hyperventilate, the room started spinning again, and then everything began to blur. I could hear Ralph calling my name, but I was unable to respond.*

I could see figures as they rushed to my bedside. The doctor was now calling my name, I wanted to respond, but it was as if someone stole my voice box. Ralph's words played in my head over and over again like a broken record before my body finally gave up and then everything went black.

"Lala, you have a phone call on line one," Shelly said snapping me out of my thoughts.

"Thank you," I said into the intercom before answering the phone. "Hello."

"Hey, bestie what's up?" Lisa chimed into the phone

"Same shit different day."

"How's my god babies?"

"They're doing fine, I'm at the clinic right now, so they're home with Anna."

"Did you see that lame ass nigga today?" she asked referring to Ralph.

"You so childish," I laughed.

"Why I gotta be all that?"

"Why you checking for my co-workers?" I joked.

"Oh, whatever! Was he with that bitch?"

"No, Lisa, he was not with Kandi."

"So, you did see him?"

"Girl, bye I got work to do. I am not about to sit here and entertain you, matter fact, hold on." I put her on hold, dialed Ralph's number, and then transferred the call. Laughing to myself, I logged into my inventory system and placed the orders for all of the items my clinics needed. I called into my other two locations and had the secretary email me all of the orders that needed to be put in the system.

When I finally finished, it was around dinnertime, so I decided to go home to my kids. Even though I was a drug dealer and business owner, I was a mother first, so I made it my priority to make it home by six in the evening every night, on the days I chose to work.

The aroma of Chili rushed me as soon as I opened the door causing my stomach to rumble. I entered the security code in the alarm and made my way to the kitchen. The kids were both sitting in their chairs with a bottle in their mouth as Anna moved around the kitchen cooking up a storm. She was a Godsend to me. Ever since Stacks' death, she had been nothing but help, every week I showed her just as much I appreciated her with a nice, hefty check every week.

I also paid her grandkids' college tuition and made sure that all of her utilities were paid on time. All she had to do was save up for her retirement. I was going to be the last family whose kids she looked after.

"Oh, Ms. Lala, you scared me," she jumped once she noticed me.

"I'm sorry, Anna, did the kids behave for you today?"

"Yes, very good. I have no problems with my babies." She smiled and kissed both of them on the cheeks.

"Good babies," I giggled and tickled them both. Although their father wasn't here to enjoy, I knew he would have been a great father.

"Sit and eat," Anna said placing a plate of Chili over a bed of white rice in front of me. This is what had me so thick; I came home to a nice, southern home cooked meal every day.

"Oh, Anna, I don't think you should be feeding the babies that."

"Oh, hush Chile, and let me feed these babies. I hope you don't think that breast milk you been pumping for them is the only thing that has them this chunky. I feed my babies." She made sure the spoon of chili was nice and cool before putting it in Amire's mouth.

After dinner, Anna cleaned up the kitchen and left for the night. I gave her two weeks of pay and informed her that I was going to be spending the following week home with the kids. She started to fuss until I gave her an all inclusive cruise trip to Jamaica for the week. Thanking me, she kissed the babies and left. I made sure that the alarm was activated before taking the kids upstairs for a bath.

One by one, I fed and burped the babies then put them to bed. I sat in the nursery with them until I was sure that they both were asleep. The stars I decorated the ceiling with lit up the room and displayed farm animals on the wall. I looked at the portrait size photo that I hung on the wall, even though Stacks was not with us in flesh, he would always be with us in spirit.

Kissing both my babies, I left their room and went to go sit in Stacks' man cave. Everything was left the same way. For some reason, being in this room brought me so much comfort. Laying down on the sofa bed, I pulled the sheets over my body and cuddled against the fabric. I could still smell his scent lingering around in the room. Praying a prayer of comfort, I asked God to allow me to dream of Stacks before I drifted off to sleep.

"Why are you crying?" a woman's voice asked.

"He's gone," I said crying over Stacks grave.

"He's not dead," she replied. I looked up and the woman looked really familiar, as she continued to walk closer to me I was able to see that it was Stacks' grandma standing next to her husband and Stacks' mother.

"Don't cry, my dear, he is not dead."

"Where is he?" I asked, but they started to fade away. "Where is he?" I yelled trying to run after them, but they were gone.

I woke up in a cold sweat trying to put together what I just dreamed. A strong felling came over me and my heart began to beat really fast. I got up and walked to the bathroom to splash water on my face. As I looked up in the mirror, I saw Stacks' face, but then it vanished.

My mind was really starting to play these fucked up tricks on me. I went downstairs and grabbed me a bottle of water. I swallowed down two pain pills and went to go check on the babies. After I changed their diapers, I laid on the daybed that was in their room and decided to do some online shopping.

I bought the kids more stuff that they didn't need then I decided to browse Amazon for some good reads. After purchasing one hundred dollars' worth of books, I decided to catch up on the Rozalyn series by Myss Shan before the finale was released December 23rd. Tamar finding out that Rozalyn fucked Brandon was the last thing I read before I fell asleep.

Chapter 2

Stacks

"Down, set, hut, hut!" I yelled passing the ball to one of my twins as he began to run with the ball. My other twin son ran after him in an attempt to tackle him down for the ball.

"Touch down!!" Justin said doing a little dance.

"No fair," Justice said with a frown. "Daddy, he cheated."

"I did not!" Justin shoved Justice.

"Hey, stop with all that, y'all brothers," I said picking Justice up. "Now, let's go get ready for bed."

We walked inside of the house and Donna was nowhere in sight. I brought the boys to the bathroom, plugged the tub, and filled it with warm water and bubbles. I sat on the edge of the tub and helped them undress before picking them up one by one and putting them in the water.

I smiled at my boys; they were everything I ever dreamed of and more. My mind wondered to Lala for a minute and my heart began to ache. Although God gave me a second chance to be with Donna and they boys, I still missed her and our twins that I never got to hold.

I still remembered that day like it was yesterday, I dreamt it every night. I was supposed to protect her and I let her down once again. I was supposed to be there to help her raise my babies, but I left her on her own to be a single mother. I was torn.

A part of me wanted to be here with Donna and the boys, but I also wanted to be with Lala. I was madly in love with Lala, she was the blood that pumped my heart.

After giving the boys their baths, I dried them off and dressed them each in a pair of Spider Man PJ's. I tucked them in bed, gave them a kiss, and read them a bedtime story until they were sound asleep. I stood there and stared at them before closing the door and walking to the bedroom I shared with Donna.

Donna was sitting there with her head in her hands while sobbing.

"What's wrong?" I asked as I sat next to her.
"It's time for you to go back," she sobbed.
"What do you mean?"
"Look at the portal?"

I looked to where she was pointing and I swear it felt like I was in a supernatural movie.

"So, why don't you and the boys come with me ma?"
"We can't, look at our skin, it's pale, we're dead. But yours still has color, it isn't your time yet."

The more she talked about this shit the more spooked a nigga became. I just sat there and held her in my arms. She continued to sob uncontrollably until she finally fell asleep. I was happy that I wasn't really dead and I had another chance of life, but I couldn't celebrate knowing that I would have to part with Donna and the twins again. I got up and went to kiss my boys goodbye, then did the same with Donna. Before I could go, my mother pulled me aside.

"Anthony, I am really proud of the man you've become." She smiled with tears in her eyes. "You blessed me with four wonderful grandchildren. Go be with your other two, it is not your time yet. I'll be here to take care of Donna and the boys."

"Thanks ma," I said holding on tightly to her. I felt her tears, which only made me bawl like a little bitch.

"It's time to go," she said as she walked me to the door. I hugged her one more time until I felt my body lift and then drop.

Opening my eyes wasn't easy to do because the light shinning from the window kept burning them. When I was finally able to adjust my eyes, I noticed that I wasn't in my house nor was I was in the hospital. My eyes wandered around the unfamiliar room taking in the scenery, there were pictures of Lala and I around the room as well as pictures of twin girls.

That threw me off a bit because I was sure as hell that I heard Lala tell me that our surprise baby was a boy. I tried to get out of the bed, but my body ached. I looked around for any sign of Lala or the babies, but there wasn't any. I heard the door open and close, feeling an uneasiness; I closed my eyes and decided to fake sleep.

Chapter 3
Amanda

"Shit!" I yelled as I dropped the baby bag while trying to carry the twins inside the house. Motherhood was a bitch I wasn't ready for. If it wasn't for me wanting to be with Stacks so bad, I wouldn't even be in this predicament. As soon as I closed the front door, Anita started to cry. I rushed and tried to get her a bottle before she woke Amita. It was a domino affect with twins, once one started to cry then the other began. Sparingly, that was not the case this time; Amita laid peacefully in her car seat as I tended to Anita.

My phone started to ring and I looked at the screen before I placed it back in my pocket. It was my cousin Tazz calling for the rest of the money I owed him for getting me the twins. His ass was out of his mind if he thought he was going to get another red cent out of me. Instead of the fool bringing me a newborn boy and girl, he brought me two girls that looked nothing like Stacks. I was just hoping whenever he did wake up out of his medically induced coma that he would be too out of it to notice.

Getting the babies settled in their crib, I walked inside of the master bedroom I shared with Stacks and began to undress. The doctor I hired to look after Stacks was here earlier and she basically told me that his vital were nice and strong, so it was basically up to him to wake up whenever his body was ready to. He looked at peace sleeping and I bent down to give him a kiss before going in the bathroom to take a shower.

I made sure the water was steamy hot before I got inside the shower. I allowed the water beads to soothe my skin as I thought back on the day I decided to make Stacks mine once and for all…

My cousin Tazz was already working with Bear and some other niggas in Flint trying to kill Stacks. I gave them the perfect day, which was the day of their baby shower. I basically orchestrated the whole thing. I had some of the men dressed up as men from a moving company that went back to Stacks' house to help them with the things from the baby shower. The plan was to run up in the house while they were sleeping, but Lala ended up going in labor.

I was on pins and needles hoping Stacks didn't die as they shot up his car. I watched from afar as they tried to resuscitate him. When they were able to do so, we highjacked the ambulance that was supposed to be bringing him to the hospital.

We removed Stacks' body and put him in my car. I set the ambulance on fire and had him airlifted to our new house in Atlanta, Georgia. He had slipped into a coma due to all the loss of blood he suffered and I was kind of happy because I had time to prepare for him when he awoke.

I hired some of the hospital's staff and had them care for him while I was out and about trying to impersonate Lala. I was able to go inside the house they once shared together and study her. I mimicked all the products she used, the scent she wore; I even stole suitcases full of her clothes and shoes.

I made Loye, Ashley's gay friend hook me up so that I resembled her. If you took a quick glance, I could pass as Lala. I just hoped Stacks was dumb enough to buy it.

The cries of the babies cut my shower short. I took a deep breath before turning the dial and grabbing my robe. I wrapped a towel around my hair and was prepared to go deal with these damn babies. UGHHHH! One was ok, but two was too much!

My heart almost stopped when I walked in the nursery and saw Stacks feeding Anita. I sat there with a lump formed in my throat; I couldn't form any words to say. I watched for a few seconds and decided to walk out of the room and allow him to bond with the babies.

Dropping my robe, I grabbed the warm, lavender body butter and began to rub it into my skin. I was a very beautiful girl, with such ugly scars due to a nasty habit. Looking in the full-length mirror, I began to inspect every scar I had due to me cutting my skin. Every scar that stained my body told a story.

"Where did all of those scars come from?" Stacks asked scaring me.

"The accident," I spoke quickly pulling on a pair of stretched pants and a baby tee.

"How old are the babies?"

"Six months."

"Man, I missed six months of my kids' life," he said to no one in particular.

"Should you be out of bed? Do you need me to call a nurse?" I asked trying to change the subject.

"Nah. I'm good." He sat on the bed looking at me "Why we ain't in Miami?"

"It was too dangerous for the kids."

"I see."

"You hungry?"

Nah. You can roll me a blunt though."

I couldn't have walked out of that room fast enough. This was too much. I wasn't expecting him to wake up so soon, and I sure as hell wasn't prepared for his line of questioning. How the fuck did he wake up so damn alert?! I silently cursed myself for not having the doctor keeping him under his medically induced coma. Now, I was forced to put on my game face and deal with this bullshit. I thought of lacing his weed with some sleeping pills, but decided against it. After numerous attempts of trying to roll the blunt, I finally ended up with a mediocre blunt that I brought to him.

"Here you go, I'm going to go start on dinner," I said handing him the blunt. I watched him as he twirled the blunt between his fingers and looked at it in disapproval.

"Bring me the wrap in the weed," was he reply. I went downstairs and gathered all the items he would need to roll his blunt and brought it back up to him with a cup and bottle of Jack Daniels. With any luck, he'd get fucked up tonight and I could avoid being interrogated.

I started seasoning the chicken for the stir-fry I was going to make. In the middle of cutting the veggies, my phone started to ring again. I sent Tazz a text letting him know that I would hit him back up later and continued prepping for dinner.

Making sure everything was well seasoned; I made sure I put my foot in this meal, ten toes and all. I made a quick garden salad and a pitcher of grape Kool-Aid to go with our meal. I made him a nice, hearty plate, added ice to his glass, and put the Kool-Aid on a tray before carrying it up to him.

"Why don't I have any clothes?" he asked as he stood in front of me naked with the blunt hanging from his mouth. He hot boxed the fuck out of the room that I was about to get high just by standing in there.

"We left in such a hurry, I really didn't have time to pack anything?"

"Word," he said laying back on the bed, dick touching the ceiling and all. My mouth began to water, so I climbed on top of him and put his dick in my mouth. I was hesitant to suck on it at first because I wasn't too sure if he was going to push me off or not.

When I felt his muscles relax, I continued to deep throat him. I was sucking my frustrations out on his dick and his light moans let me know that he was enjoying it. I used my throat and tightened it around his dick, causing him to grab the back of my head for mercy.

I licked his shaft, kissed the tip of his dick, and continued to bless him with the best head I had ever given. Curling my lips, I made sure my teeth made no contact as I assaulted his dick with my vicious mouth. After swallowing a set of his twins, I climbed on top of him, pulled off my shorts, and began to ride him. I bent down and tried to give him a kiss, however, he wouldn't kiss me back. Instead, he bit and sucked on my neck as he pumped in and out of me.

Stacks flipped me over and started fucking me from the back. I was moaning out his name and throwing this ass back at him matching his every thrust.

"Shiiiiiiiiiiit!" I hissed as I felt my orgasm build up. He continued to fuck me with no mercy causing my pussy to squirt all over his dick. I felt him release his seeds in me before he collapsed next to me and tried to catch his breath.

"You ok?" I asked.

"Yeah, I'm good. Go grab me some shit to wear, I don't plan on walking around naked all day," he said getting up and walking towards the bathroom. "Leave the twins!"

I couldn't understand why he was being so short and snappy with me. Shrugging my shoulders, I grabbed a Summer's Eve wipes, cleaned my pussy, and got dressed. The twins were both asleep in their beds, so I didn't want to disturb them. I turned on the baby monitor and left the house.

Chapter 4

Lala

"You sure you're ok with them for the night?" I asked Anna. Tonight was Ralph's birthday party at Club X and I really wanted to throw it up with my new right hand, but as a mother, my kids came first.

"Baby, you fine go turn up," she said trying to twerk.

"Oh, Lawd, Ms. Anna, don't give me too much," I laughed.

"What you mean? Back in my day, I used to be a real bad bitch, hell I'm still one now."

I kicked it with Anna before I drove to Lisa's house, so we could get ready together.

Using my keys, I opened the door and she was already turning up. The music was blasting and she had a blunt in one hand and a cup in another. I grabbed the blunt out of her hand and joined her. We were both bouncing our ass to the Miami Jiggle while we passed the weed back and fourth.

Three blunts and four songs later, we deiced to get ready. I was high as fuck as I dressed in an all black body suit. The whole back was exposed displaying my plump ass. The front had a drop neck that my huge boobs courtesy of the twins held in place.

I paired it with my knee high black and gold Louis Vuitton pumps and added my gold chain, gold Gucci watch, and earrings. I twirled in the mirror admiring my postpartum figure; my babies had done me great. Grabbing the Escada perfume, I sprayed my body and went downstairs to wait on Lisa.

I was on my third cup of Pink Moscato when Lisa finally finished getting ready. I was mad until I saw her outfit; my girl was out for the kill. I stood and applauded her as she stood in front of me wearing an all white short Prada dress. Her ass was on a planet of its on and she wore a pair of white and gold Prada pumps on her feet. Her inches were in big curls and her makeup was done to perfection.

She smelt like warm vanilla and I was pretty sure she added some of that special sweet mix to her pussy. She was determined to get Ralph on her team and I was down for it.

"No panties?" I asked watching her ass jiggle as she walked around the house gathering the rest of her things

"What I need panties for?" she winked and grabbed the glass out of my hand and drunk my liquor. We sat and sipped some more before we got in my brand new candy apple Audi. I had developed this obsession with cars; I think it was my way of dealing with Stacks being gone. Whatever it was had my built in parking garage looking like a car show.

When we arrived on the scene, I just nodded my head and we were granted entrance. I now ran the streets of Miami, so I held a lot of respect. The bodyguards that I hired met me by the door and cleared a path for us to make it to the VIP section. I had bodyguards everywhere; I wasn't taking any chance, especially not with my children. I knew what I was doing when I signed up for this lifestyle, so it was up to me to play it smart. I was a very observant person, so it didn't take long for me to catch on. I just followed everything Stacks did and added things that he should have done.

"Happy birthday, Ralph!" I said giving him a hug and handing him his gift. "Hey Kandi," I greeted her not wanting to be rude.

"Thanks ma," he said before grabbing the box and opening it. "Damn ma, you wild," he said as he smiled at all the different foreign watches I'd bought him. I had them all displayed in a diamond-encrusted case. His gift cost me a pretty penny, but he was worth it. I couldn't have asked for a better partner.

"Happy birthday, Ralph," Lisa finally said giving him a hug and kiss. "I'll give you your present later," she smirked and winked at Kandi. Not wanting anything to escalate, I grabbed Lisa's hand and dragged her to the dance floor.

The DJ was spinning Nicki Minaj's *Stupid Hoe* and the club was going bananas. Lisa looked Kandi in the eyes as she sung the words of the lyrics. I tried my hardest not to laugh, but I couldn't, Lisa was really going hard in the paint. The song finally switched to Lil Wayne's *I'm Going In*. I got real hyped as I rapped the lyrics to the song and started throwing money. It felt real good to get out the house and turn up and I was really enjoying myself. Ralph joined me on the dance floor and we turned up.

> *"Hold up, wait one motherfuckin' minute*
> *It's the El Capitan, I got motherfuckin' lieutenant*
> *If I said I'm going in, then I motherfuckin' meant it*
> *And if I brought it in the club, then I'mma*
> *motherfuckin' spend it"*

When Jeezy's part came on, I had to rap along with him. I put my arm around my motherfucking lieutenant Ralph and together we made it thunderstorm. I thought about my soul mate Stacks and smiled up to the heavens at him. I knew this was how he showed out when they went out and I was happy that I could somewhat be that homeboy to Ralph even though I was a female.

"Can the birthday boy please report to the stage?" Ralph looked at me for answers, but all I did was shrug. Lisa was my best friend and I was not about to say nothing, but I was going to sit back and enjoy the show. I laughed a little as I watched him slowly walk up the stage.

I took a seat in VIP next to Kandi because I wanted to see her facial expression. Ralph finally made it to the stage and was seated on a seat that was designated for him. The lights went low and Usher's new song *I Don't Mind* started blasting.

Shawty, I don't mind if you dance on a pole
That don't make you a ho
Shawty, I don't mind when you work until three
If you're leaving with me
Go make that money, money, money
Your money, money, money
Cause I know how it is, go and handle your biz

And get that money, money, money

Your money, money, money

You can take off your clothes

Long as you coming home, girl, I don't mind

Lisa came out in a sexy ass two-piece set with a mask covering her face. She began dancing on the pole that sat directly in front of Ralph. She then flipped and landed on his lap and started grinding on him. She was whispering in his ears and by the way his body relaxed, I could tell that she revealed to him her identity. I read her lips tell him to listen to the words of the song before she finished up her dance routine for him. Kandi was looking real sick in the face, so I decided to get up and bring her a drink.

"Anything she wants is on the house," a voice said as soon as I finished ordering the drinks for our section.

"I can pay for my..." I turned around ready to snap until I saw the face of the dude. I was speechless. I kept pinching myself trying to make sure I wasn't dreaming. I wanted to make sure that I was actually looking in the face of Idris Elba.

"Hey, I'm Joey," he greeted me. I was able to finally let go of the breath I was holding when I realized that he didn't have that British accent and that his name was different.

"I bet you thought I was Idris Elba," he laughed.

"Yes, I did," I admitted and laughed with him.

"No, I'm just Joey who happens to strongly resemble the dude," he said straightening his black Gucci vest. He was Gucci down in all black adding more to his sex appeal. I grabbed one of the drinks and drowned them down as I began to have naughty thoughts of the dude.

"What's your name?" he asked breaking the silence.

"Lala," I blushed

"Lala. That's eccentric."

"How are you enjoying yourself?"

"I'm having a blast, this club is amazing!"

"Thank you," he smiled.

"Is this your club?"

"Yes, it is, we just opened it five months ago."

"We?"

"My brothers and I."

"That's good."

"Well, I know you want to get back to your friends, here's my card, give me a call. I'd love to take you out to lunch."

I took his card and stared at it before putting it in my small gold clutch.

"Will do," he ordered one of the waitresses to bring my drinks back to the table for me. I smiled and walked back to the VIP section where all eyes were on me.

"What?" I innocently asked.

"Don't what nothing bitch! Why you ain't bring Idris fine ass back to the table?" Lisa asked.

"That was Joey."

"Well Joey, Mikey, Franky, or whoever that was can get it!" I looked over at Ralph and saw him low key hating on what Lisa just said. He was showing some type of jealously.

"Girl just chill," I said pouring another drink. For the rest of the night, there were no bad vibes as we ate, smoke, drank, and enjoyed each other's company. Although Kandi was sitting there with us, it was like she didn't matter. I kind of felt bad for her, but hey she was at war with my best friend and I was team Lisa all day every day.

***

The next morning, I woke up to Amire screaming at the top of his lungs. I regretted allowing Anna to go home as soon as I got here. I quickly splashed water on my face and walked in the nursery.

Amiracle was still sleeping, so I took him to the kitchen with me to make him some breakfast. Anna had him so hooked on food that he barely wanted the bottle anymore. I made them both some oatmeal and pureed it. When Amire was done with his second bowl, Amiracle was just waking up. I fed her, and then took them to the bathroom for a nice warm bath.

I poured some lavender Johnson and Johnson in their tub. I sat Amire in his rocker as I gave Amiracle her bath first. When I was done, I rotated and gave Amire his bath. I dressed them down in matching Jordan outfits and put them down for their nap.

The house was clean, laundry was done, and the house was filled with groceries thanks to Anna. So the only thing left for me to do was relax. Pouring me a glass of red wine, I sat in my hot bubble bath and allowed the jets in the tub to take care of my body.

I let my body soak for a good thirty minutes before rinsing off and making me some breakfast. Before I could take a bite of my bacon, Amire was up again crying. I picked him up and brought him back to the kitchen with me. Handing him a piece of bacon to nibble on, I ate my breakfast.

It was still hard for me to believe that I had twins. The doctors had no clue I had two babies in me and neither did I. When I asked the doctor how was this possible, she told me that sometimes because the second baby is way smaller than the first baby, it is very easy for the baby to hide behind the other.

That explained why Amire was born way smaller than Amiracle, he also had a few problems at birth, but he was much better now and bigger, too. I guess he was making up for all the food he didn't get to eat in my womb.

After we finished breakfast, I laid him across my chest as we watched cartoons. My mind wandered to Joey, so I got up to retrieve his number from my clutch. Punching it in my keypad, I decided to give him a call.

"Hello," he groggily answered the phone.

"Did I wake you?" I sweetly asked.

"No, you did not Lala."

"How did you know it was me?"

"I never forget a sweet voice."

"Is that so?"

"Yes, Ma'am."

I guess Amire was getting jealous of mommy flirting on the phone because he decided to cry.

"You have a baby?" his sexy ass voice boomed through the phone.

"Yes, I have twins actually," I said getting up and walking up to the nursery. "Do you have any children?" I asked as I placed Amire on the changing table and prepared to change his diaper.

"Yes, I have a twelve-year-old daughter and a eight month old son."

"How old are you?"

"42. Why? Am I too old for you?"

"No. I was just asking."

I finished up with Amire and put him in his baby rocker. I then went to go check on Amiracle, she was wet, so I changed her and put her in her rocker. I sat on the floor Indian style and watched my babies rock back and forth as I continued my conversation with the very sexy Joey. Our conversation was on a whole different level and I was enjoying it until the other line of my phone beeped. I wanted to ignore it, but it was Stacks' father, so I had to answer.

"Hola, Papa," I answered.

"Subir a un avión y venir aquí ahora!(get on a plane and come here now!)" he roared through the phone before he hung it up.

I started to call Anna and ask her to watch the babies for me, but decided against it. The last time they saw their grandfather was when they were four months old. Plus if I was in any trouble with him, the kids would probably soften him up a bit.

I got up and sent Joey a quick 'I'll talk to you later text' and went to pick the kids clothes out. I grabbed the large Fendi baby bag and packed the kids clothes and the other necessities that they would need on our mini trip. I decided to dress Amiracle in a white dress, with a blue dress shirt that had blue polka dots all over it.

I tied the mini, brown baby leather belt around her waist and put some brown leather boots on her tiny feet. I brushed all of her pretty hair in a neat high bun and put a brown bow around it. I dressed Amire different from his sister, although they were twins, I wanted them to have their own identity so every so often, I would dress them differently.

A pair of black Tommy jeans, a red button down Tommy shirt, a fresh out the box pair of red, black, and white Jordan's topped his outfit off. Smiling at my kids, I snapped a few pictures and went to get dressed.

Dressed in a pair of khaki high waist pants, a white shirt and a pair of leopard print Gucci heels, I brushed my long weave down my back and applied some gloss. I loaded the items in my Mercedes truck and went back in the house to retrieve the kids.

After I was sure that they were securely buckled, I turned on the TV and Barney instantly filled the speakers. Nodding to my guards, I gave them detailed instructions a pulled off.

The ride to the airport was a fifteen-minute drive. I checked the baby mirrors and made sure that they were ok. When I arrived, I parked my card in my reserved parking spot. The pilot came over and helped me board the plane with the kids. I was glad I had a private plane that I could use to come and go as I pleased. I wasn't really in the mood to deal with all the havoc that came with riding the regular plane, especially now that I had kids.

I sent Stacks' father a text to let him know that we boarded the plane. When we landed, a car was already there waiting for us. The driver came and assisted me with putting the kids in the car. The whole drive to the mansion, I kept thinking what was so urgent that Stacks' father wanted me to drop everything and come see him.

While my mind was in a frenzy trying to figure out what could possibly be wrong, we were pulling up in the circular driveway. No matter how many times I came over, I always fell in love with the mansion all over again.

"Mis adorables nietos (my lovely grandchildren)," Stacks father said as he grabbed them out of my hand as soon as we got inside. He carried them to the family room and sat in his favorite chair. He complimented me on how well the looked. I thanked him and sat across from him. I had to smile at myself; I was really doing a great job at motherhood. After playing with the kids for a good half an hour, he called out for his housekeeper to take them.

"Qué carajo estabas pensando, Lala? (What the fuck were you thinking Lala?)" Stack's father asked.

"¿De Que estás hablando de papá? (What are you talking about papa?)" I replied.

After Stacks' father gave me the job of taking Stacks' place, he made sure I had all the proper training I needed. I was taught how to kill a man with my bare hands, shoot in the dark, and hit my targets, cut, cook, and taste for good quality drugs. I also learned Spanish, which I was now fluently speaking along side of French.

"¿Poe qué convertir Carla en su enemigo? Esteems suponemos estar trabajando juntos para evitar la guerra!

(Why would you turn Carla into your enemy? We are supposed to be working together to avoid war!)" he angrily snapped. I could see his face turn a shade of red.

"Papa CAD movement Que hago está bien calculado. Hay una razón detrás de todo lo que hago, nunca me pongo una guerra sin razón. (Papa every move I make is well calculated. There is a reason behind everything I do, I would never start a war for no reason.)"

"Explique. Estoy escuchando. (Explain. I am listening.)"

"Puedo mostrarle mejor que te puedo decir. (I can show you better than I can tell you.)" I replied taking out my iPad.

I showed him all of the numbers Stacks was bringing in while he was still here, then I showed him the numbers I was bringing in. I was bringing in more money on my side with Ralph than I was with Carla, however, Carla had access to more product and she had the good territory. I showed him how Ralph numbers were going up and how Carla numbers kept decreasing.

"I see," he replied after my presentation.

"See papa I would never cause any unnecessary drama. I have kids to protect."

"I understand. Do what needs to be done."

"I intend to."

After a long day of shopping, the kids and I finally returned back to the States. I cursed Stacks' father under breath as it took me hours to unload all the things he bought for the kids. When I was finally done, my body was beyond exhausted.

I sent out emails to check on my clinics and made a reminder to catch up with Lisa. The house was finally nice and quiet and I was just getting ready to get in bed before Stacks' office phone rang. I was too tired to move, so I decided to go to bed and retrieve the missed call the following morning.

Chapter 5

Bear

It felt good to be king. I was doing the damn thing in Flint. After we offed that nigga Stacks, I killed Alan and made it looked like he died in the crossfire. He had another thing coming if he thought I was going to let his ass leave Miami alive for the stunt that he pulled.

Since the day he set me free, I had a few bullets with his name on it. I just needed him to help me take out Stacks first. With Alan now out the way, I was able to take over the city, and his bitch. I was using his workers, to push work, while his wife was on her knees sucking my dick better than Supa Head.

My fresh out the box pair of royal, purple Tims hit the pavement as I exited the plane. A nigga was definitely looking like Rick Ross, my head was shaved and shined, and my beard was full. I had on a pair of army fatigue pants, a purple polo, and a pair of black Gucci shades on my face.

I threw my Gucci book bag around my back and walked up the street to the car rental shop. The big diamond chunk that hung around my neck shined in the Miami sun making every bitch I walked past pussy wet. It'd been a minute since I was in Miami and with Stacks dead; I had plans on taking over his shit, as well.

"Welcome to Hertz, how may I help you," Snow White asked with a pretty as smile as soon as I walked in.

"I need the flyest car you have and your phone number." I pulled my shades off to inspect the white girl that was walking around in a black girl's body.

She blushed then wrote her number down on the back of a card for me. I slapped her fat ass as she walked past me in search for my request. A few minutes later, she pulled up in the front driving a 2014 all white Escalade truck. It wasn't really my style, but I'd fuck with it until I was able to get to my man Biz and cop me some fly shit. I signed the paperwork and she handed me the keys.

"How long will you be needing the car?" she asked.

"Not long. As soon as I have your ass tooted up in the backseat fucking your brains out, you can take the car back," I smirked.

"Don't lose my number," she smiled.

"Trust me I won't." I looked her up and down one more time before getting in the car and driving off.

I knew I was going to have to lay low for a little bit until I got rid of Ralph's ass. I still couldn't believe how much Stacks' bitch ass put that nigga on. Good thing his ass was now taking a permanent dirt nap. I made a memo to locate his gravesite just so I could piss all over his bitch ass.

I pulled up to the Hilton Beach resort and checked in the presidential suite. Sitting on the balcony, I rolled me a few blunts of the loud and poured me a cup of Remy. Pulling out my iPhone, I called up my lil nigga Tazz.

"What's good fam?" he answered.

"Nothing just coolin'."

"You in the city?"

"Yea boy, where you at?"

"I had to check my peoples in Georgia, but I should be on that side in a few days."

"Cool. Check me out. Swing by Flint and make sure my shit straight before you come on this end."

"Iight.'"

Tazz was a lil nigga from Alan's camp that had heart and was loyal. This nigga was down for any and everything. I had to make that nigga my right hand after the way he set the ambulance that was trying to rescue Stacks on fire.

Although he had proven himself to me, I always stayed a step ahead of him. I had trust issues with everyone including myself. Stacks trusted me and I was the reason he was dead. So for me to put my trust in a nigga or a bitch was a no-no.

The effects of the weed were making my dick hard, so I pulled out my phone and watched a few porn videos. The way them white chicks was swallowing the dick made me think of lil mama I met today. I decided to call up the snow bunny and see if she was fucking or not.

Chapter 6

Stacks

Something about the situation I was in didn't seem right. Somebody was playing a sick joke with me and I wasn't with this shit. Swabbing the twins' mouth, I put it in an envelope and gave it to the mailman as soon as he came. I grabbed the mail and looked at the names, nothing was addressed to Lala, which made the situation even crazier.

I wasn't a dumb nigga. I knew this wasn't Lala and the twins weren't mine. I still wanted to have them tested because something I would never do was turn my back on my kids no matter what.

I sat at the table a rolled me a blunt. I waited until the kids fell asleep and started to ease my mind. With every toke I took, shit began to become clear to me. I knew the sick bitch behind this shit was Amanda. For one, her pussy wasn't on Lala's level.

Lala's pussy was a perfect fit to my dick. Amanda had good pussy, but the fit wasn't there. Another thing was the way she rolled my blunt. Lala never rolled me just one uneven ass blunt, she always made sure I had multiple blunts rolled. I didn't know why Amanda thought that she was going to be able to pull this shit off, but I had a bullet with her name on it.

Lala had all of her numbers changed, the only number that stayed the same was my office number and I was having a hard time trying to reach her. I was tired of calling, so I decided to call Ralph instead.

"Who dis?!" he answered.

"Nigga it ain't no bitch," I replied.

The phone line went silent.

"Stacks?"

"The one and only."

"Nigga I-"

"You thought what? I was dead? Nah, real niggas don't die, we kick it with Jesus for a few months then come back home," I joked.

"Where you at?"

"In Atlanta, Georgia or some shit." I could hear Amanda's car in the driveway, so I decided to cut the call short, I didn't want her to know I was onto her ass. "Yo' but check it, stay by this phone and in a few days I'mma call you to come get me. Don't tell Lala though."

"I got you fam. Be easy."

"One," I said hanging up and stuffing the phone in my pocket before she could open the door.

I watched her as she walked towards me; this girl was really fucked up in the head. She transformed herself completely just so that she could look like Lala. To any other fool this would have worked, but I was too in tune with Lala to not know Amanda was a fake. I wanted to jump on her ass and beat her to death, but that wasn't my style. As soon as I got to the bottom of this shit, I was bodying her ass and whoever helped her.

"Hey baby," she said walking towards me.

"Sup," I said and looked in her the face. "So, when you think shit will blow over enough for me to go back to the city? It's been a month!"

"Your dad wants us to give it some time."

"You spoke with my pops?"

"Yes," she lied with a straight face.

"When was this?"

"Just a few minutes ago."

"Why you ain't let me talk to him?"

"We barely spoke as if you was alive, whoever after us is still lurking. Trust me baby, I got it all under control." She smiled and kissed me on the lips. My dick didn't even jump like the way it did when I kissed Lala.

The twins started to cry and I watched how she rolled her eyes on the low before getting up to attend to their needs. While she was gone, I grabbed her phone and started to look through it. Her messages were empty, but there were a lot of calls in her log from a person name Tazz.

I grabbed a pen and quickly wrote down the number. I looked for any more clues, but came up empty. Putting the number in my pocket, I smoked another joint and thought of Lala. The real one.

I wondered if her and the kids were ok. I knew they were straight financially because of my father and Ralph, plus I left her and the kids everything I had, which was a little over 1.1 billion dollars.

She came back holding a twin in each hand. I grabbed one of the babies out of her hand and held her. She was a cute little girl, but I did not feel the connection I felt when I held my daughter the day of the accident.

"When are their birthdays?" I asked.

"February 3rd," she hesitantly replied.

"I definitely knew she was way off, the babies were born the night of Lala baby's shower, which was March 20th.

"Cool," I replied handing her the baby and going to go sit out on the porch. I knew for sure that this bitch wasn't my wife and those kids wasn't mine and as soon as the DNA results came, I was going to beat her ass silly with them before ending her miserable life once and for all.

Chapter 7
Ralph

Hearing my dawg's voice fucked me up in the head. To say a nigga was surprised was an understatement. I ain't know how Lala was going to take this news, but that shit she had going on with that new nigga she'd been seeing would have to cease before Stacks got home.

It was something about that Joey nigga that rubbed me the wrong way. They day she invited us to dinner so that we could meet I was getting nothing but bad vibes from him. I was a very observant nigga, so I was going to watch his ass close.

I watched Kandi pack her bags and I was kind of happy that she was leaving. Her semester of school was about to start in a few days, so she had to head back to New York. I'd been kicking it with her lightly since Lisa and I called quits.

My head was still gone off Lisa, but my pride wouldn't allow me to fuck with her like that. I lost count of all the times I had to go upside a nigga head for talking sideways about her being a stripper.

As I watched Kandi move across the room, I couldn't help but compare her to Lisa. She was so soft spoken, whereas Lisa was a firecracker. Lisa was the type of bitch every boss nigga needed. She knew how to be a lady in the streets, a freak in the sheets, and a boss bitch when I needed one.

I had no doubt in my mind that Lisa was built for a nigga like me. Kandi was just too fragile. Dealing with her was like dealing with a child and I was too grown to be trying to fuck with a bitch who wasn't on my level. I knew our days of kicking it were close to being over. I just hoped like hell she wasn't one of those crazy bitches who couldn't handle rejection.

"Are you going to come visit me?" she asked snapping me out of my thoughts.

"We'll see."

"Why?" she asked poking her lips out. This is the shit I couldn't stand. She ain't know how to put on her big girl panties and give me space.

"I have to work."

"Oh, that's what you call it."

"Yes, that's what the fuck I call it. It pays the bills, right? It buys you all this name brand shit, pays for your expensive ass fashion school, and keep your ass in all the flyest rides! Don't question shit I do when you benefiting from it!" I yelled before walking out the house.

I jumped in my car and drove around. Usher's new song started playing on the radio, the beat was fye, so I decided to funk to it for a little bit. I was listening to the words of the song and it made a lot on sense.

Pulling up in front of Lisa's house, I grabbed the pre rolled blunt and sparked it up. I knew she was home by all the movement that was going on in the house. I saw two figures through the blinds. They looked too close for it to be Lala plus her car wasn't anywhere in sight. Rage instantly filled my veins when I thought of the possibility of her being with another nigga.

I finished my blunt and got out the car. I tried to use my key, but she had the locks changed. Bawling up my fist, I banged on the door as if I was an officer of Miami Dade.

"Who the fuck is-" Lisa said opening the door but froze once she realized it was me. "What do you want, Ralph?"

"I need to wait on a tow truck, my car acting funny," I lied.

"What's wrong with your car?"

"It won't start. You gon' let me in or not?" I said licking my lips and admiring the way her ass was sitting nice in her jeans.

"I have company."

"What that gotta do with me?"

"Behave," she said and opened the door wide enough for me to enter.

I walked in the house and saw this square ass nigga standing in the hallway.

"I'mma be upstairs," I said and sized up the nigga as I walked to her room. I kicked off my shoes and got in her bed making myself comfortable. My phone was ringing off the hook; I looked and saw Kandi's name flashing across the screen, so I turned off my personal phone and left my business phone on just in case Lala needed me. Grabbing the remote, I put it on re-runs of the The Wayan's Brothers.

"You ain't shit!" Lisa said hitting me in the head with a pillow.

"What you mean? I'm chillin' and watching TV."

"You know what the fuck I mean!"

"Yeah whatever, where ol'boy at?"

"He left!"

"Damn he a square for real. A real Boss nigga would have came up here and told me to clear it. Stop fucking with these lames ma."

"How long the tow truck gon be?"

"I don't know I never called one."

"You make me sick," she said and walked towards the bathroom. A few minutes later, I heard the shower turn on. The smell of watermelons seeped through the cracks of the door as she handled her hygiene.

I got up and went in the kitchen in search of something to eat. Grabbing some sub rolls, I made both of us some roast beef subs. Plating the food, I put it on a tray with a big bag of Lays, two grape Fantas, and a few blunts I had rolled.

As I was walking in the room, Lisa was walking out the bathroom. I bumped into her by mistake and caused her towel to fall. My eyes roamed all over her body before she could snatch the towel off the ground and cover up.

"What you hiding your body for?"
"This ain't for your eyes to see."

I sat the food on the bed and grabbed a sub. "Come sit and eat," I said before taking a big bite of the sub while stuffing some chips in my mouth. I watch her lotion up her body and slip a longer summer dress over her head before joining me. Picking up her sub, we ate in silence.

"What you doing here?" she asked in between bites.

"I came to see you."

"Why, ain't yo bitch at home?"

"I ain't got a bitch, but if you're referring to Kandi, I fuck with her but ain't no titles on what we doing."

"What are y'all doing?"

"We just fucking around, nothing more nothing less."

"I guess."

"You know you still feeling the kid," I said downing the soda before I fired up the blunt.

"Naw, kid you still feeling me."

"You right."

When we were done eating, Lisa got up to bring the plates in the kitchen. I shook off the sheets making sure to get rid of any crumbs before laying back down.

"Come lay on daddy's chest." I motioned for her to come over to me. "Did you fuck him?" I asked and lifted her so that she was laying on top of me.

"How, when you came in here cock blocking and shit."

"So, why did you jump in the shower?"

"I didn't know I needed permission to wash my ass."

"Why your mouth so smart?"

"Cuz' I'm a smart bitch."

We laid in bed in silence. The sound of her heartbeat matched mine to the T. One day, I was going to make this chick my wife, she was going to have my children, and we was gon' grow old together. I kissed her on the forehead before closing my eyes and falling asleep.

Chapter 8
Lala

"Five. Six. Seven. Eight. Hold it, hold it. You're almost there. Nine. Ten. Shake it off," Joey said as he coached me. We were at the build in gym that he had at his house and he was working me out like he did three times a week. My body was so sore and I was ready to throw in the towel.

"Here drink this," he said and tossed me a bottle of water. I drowned the whole thing in one huge gulp.

"Damn that was an intense workout," I said trying to catch my breath.

"Yeah, it was crazy, I'm happy you ain't give up, I like that," he smiled before he threw me a towel.

"I never give up," I replied as I eyed his deep, chocolate muscles. The way his sweat was dripping causing them to glisten had me feeling some type of way. I took another gulp of water trying to cool my kitty down.

"You see something you like?"

"Possibly."

"As a child, my mother always told me to go for what I wanted to avoid regrets."

"Wise woman."

"That she is," he said eyeing my body in my spandex workout suit. "You're more than welcome to go shower in here. I'll go start on lunch."

"Ok." I grabbed my pink and black Nike bag and entered the bathroom.

Shedding my body of the sweaty workout clothes, I stepped on the cold tile shower floor. I made sure the water was steamy hot before I adjusted the showerhead so that the water would be falling all over me. I stood in the water and allowed the heat from the water to caress my aching muscles before grabbing my ginger tea shampoo and washing my hair.

My inches were the real deal, I bought them in the best hair boutique in Columbia, so I didn't have to worry about it falling apart.

When I finished my hair, I applied my face cream and proceeded to lathering my body with the Coast body wash. Satisfied with how clean my skin was, I allowed the water to rinse my body clean. Wrapping the large, black cherry cloth towel around my body, I started to blow dry the five thousand dollar extensions I had in my hair.

Pulling my hair in a ponytail, I grabbed the coco butter body oil and rubbed it all over my legs stopping at the tattoo I got three months ago. It was a tattoo with a large heart holding a stack of money that read, *Forever lady Stacks.* I was preoccupied with rubbing my tattoo that I didn't hear the tap on the door.

"Lala, are you ok," Joey asked.

"Yes, I'm fine just getting dressed," I said wiping the tears that were now falling.

"Ok. Lunch is ready."

"I'll be out in a sec."

Whispering a prayer of strength, I dressed in a long black maxi dress. I put the diamond studs Stacks bought me in my ears along with the matching bracelet. I slipped my feet in my Michael Kors sandals, grabbed all my things, and stuffed them in my duffel bag.

As I neared the kitchen, I could smell the food Joey was preparing. He was standing next to the stove shirtless, in a pair of black sweat pants, drinking a glass of what I assumed was a shake. The way his muscles flexed every time he lifted the glass to his lips to take a sip had my kitty doing flips.

"It's rude to stare," he said noticing me salivating over him.

"I didn't mean to be rude."

"You're good." He flashed me with a smile that almost made me pass out. "Take a seat," he said motioning toward the table.

I sat down and he brought two plates over to the table with two bottles of water. I gave grace before positioning my napkin across my lap and picking up my fork.

"It smells good, what is this?" I asked.
"Its veggie stuffed zucchini."

I was hesitant to try to the food at first, but when the food hit my tongue and my taste buds got a hold of it, I was singing a different tune.

"This is really good," I complimented before taking another bite.
"Thank you. Nothing like a great meal to back up a great workout."
"Thanks again for helping me tone up."

"No need, the pleasure is all mine," he flirted and flashed me another one of those orgasmic smiles.

During lunch, we ate and made small talk. Joey was so intelligent and he always seemed to stimulate my mind. He differed from James and Stacks. Maybe because he was a legit businessman versus being a king pin. Whatever it was he was slowly pulling me in. While helping Joey clean the kitchen, my phone started to ring. Looking down at it I started to push ignore until I saw Stacks' father calling. Drying my hand, I slid my finger across the screen.

"Hola, papa," I answered.

"Necesito que vayas mango Carla ahora! (I need you to go handle Carla now!)" he angrily shouted before hanging up the phone. I sent Ralph a text telling him to meet me at the house in fifteen minutes.

"I'm sorry to have to cut this short, but I have a family emergency," I said as I faced Joey.

"Is everything ok?"

"It will be. I'll call you." I gave him a hug. As soon as our bodies touched, it was like a jolt of electricity shot through my body. It felt so good to be in someone's arms that I wanted to just lay there. Gathering the strength I needed, I broke our embrace. Picking up my duffle bag, he walked me to the car where we made promises to see each other later before I pulled off.

The guards had the gate opened for me, so I pulled in and saw Ralph waiting for me on my front porch.

"What's up did, Papa fill you in?" I asked.

"Yes, where were you?" he asked giving me the side eye.

"Really, Ralph?" I asked keying in the code to the front door. It was the same code Stacks showed me. For some reason, I was able to change everything about the house, but didn't want to change the code.

"What did Carla do?" I asked steering a way from his line of questioning.

"She's been stealing money and drugs. Papa was able to have an undercover working with her to monitor her every move. She's bringing in four times more than what the numbers say on paper."

"Suit the men up, we're making a trip," I said stomping up the stairs. I was pissed, I knew this bitch was playing dirty, but I didn't know she was this dirty. Not only was she making the profits, she was making more than expected and not even giving us our cut, which was the agreement we made.

I walked inside of Stacks' office, which I had extended and turned into a his/hers office. I needed an office space, however I didn't want to get rid of none of Stacks' things. I planned on holding onto everything for as long as I possibly could.

Powering on my MacBook Pro, I made reservations for Anna, the kids and her family at the Disney hotel. I was going to send them on vacation for a month until everything had blown over. I emailed her all the reservation information, scheduled to have a car pick them up, and wired her enough money to last them.

When I was done, I packed them each a bag of the all the things they would need before sitting it by the door.

Putting the code in my gun case, I pulled out my two favorite guns and placed them on the table. I zipped up my bulletproof vest and buttoned up my all black Versace silk blouse. Wiggling in a pair of black Versace slacks, I made sure my blouse was neatly tucked inside before wrapping a black belt around my waist.

I put my French pedicured toes in my black pumps, and then put my arms through my black vest. I positioned one of my guns in the small of my back and the other I placed in my purse. Printing some paperwork from the computer, I neatly put them in my briefcase and made my way out the door.

"Look at Columbiana," Ralph laughed.

"Shut up and let's go, we have to make a stop at Anna's," I said calling Anna and letting her know I was on the way.

"What you pushing today?" Ralph asked.

"My all black Lincoln LS."

"Dressed in all black, huh?"

"And you know this mane," I said trying my best to imitate Chris Tucker.

When we arrived in front of Anna's two-story brick house, I went inside to say hello to my babies. Picking each of them up, I played with them and kissed them on their chubby cheeks. I told Anna about their trip and she was happy. She kept thanking me when I should have been the one thanking her for agreeing to watch my babies for a month.

I wanted to cry when it was time for me go, but decided not to. I took a look at Amire and gave him another kiss; he was my real miracle baby because I had no idea I was carrying him. Being in his presence really warmed my heart because he was a spitting image of his father.

Young Jeezy's *Thug Motivation 101* CD was bumping through the speakers as we made our way to Doral. When we arrived, I made my way to all of Carla's traps and shut them all down, taking all the money and drugs with me. After cleaning out the traps, I made my way to their family's home.

"How may I help you?" the guard asked.

"I'm here to see señor Carl and señorita Carla."

"One minute."

After waiting for ten minutes, the gates finally unlocked and I was granted access. Parking my car in the circular driveway, we walked to the front door where we were frisked. The jackass the frisked me was too busy trying to feel on my ass that he didn't notice the gun in the small of my back.

"To what do I owe this visit?" Carl asked once he met us in the foyer.

"I'm here to tell you that we are no longer interested in doing business with you or your daughter."

"And who made this decision?"

"I did. After your daughter broke your end of the deal. Profits from this territory was supposed to be split with us and for some reason your daughter has been seeing money that we aren't."

"I see," he said scratching his head. "Well, how can we fix this?"

"It's a done deal. It cannot be fixed. Your family is no longer in the loop and the territory is ours." I reached in the briefcase and handed him the papers. "To avoid conflict, I am willing to buy you out."

He took the papers, ripped them, and then threw them in my face.

"Do you know what this mean?"

"It means, I am taking my business away from you, your city will dry up because I am the connect. So, if you want to still benefit you should really pick up the pieces of that contract, locate the dotted line, and sign it!"

"You little black bitch."

"That's Ms. Black Bitch to you, wetback."

"Padre esa pequeña perra negro ha perdido la razón (father that little black bitch has lost her mind)," Carla said as she stormed in the room not even noticing that I was standing here.

"I may be a bitch, but you will respect me," I smirked catching her off guard. She tried to smack me, so I punched her in the nose causing her to fly backwards and crash into the glass table. At the moment, the guards started rushing in with their guns drawn. Ralph simply hit a button on his cell phone and all of my men were waiting, surrounding the whole house with guns drawn, as well. They had about ten men, but that was no match for the twenty I came with not including the snipers. I was a well-prepared woman.

"This is going to turn really messy unless you advise your men to get their guns out of my fucking face!" I snapped.

Carl made a hand signal and everyone simultaneously dropped their guns except Ralph, who was still standing there with a gun in each hand. One of the guards went to help Carla off the floor, giving her a rag to hold up against her nose that was now gushing blood.

"Now, the offer no longer stands. Your days of pushing weight in Miami are over. No connect will deal with you and no one will work these blocks for you. A little word of advice, never bite the hands of the little black bitch who feeds you!" I snapped and like the boss bitch I was, I walked out of the house not even looking back.

"Look at Columbiana handling business."

"Shut up Ralph and take me home," I said tossing him the keys.

"On the real though, what's up with you and dude?" he asked.

"Nothing we just chilling."

"I don't trust his ass."

"Why not?"

"I'm good at reading people and he's a snake."

"Ralph, Stacks is gone. I'm going to have to move on at some point of my life," I replied.

He looked as if he was going to say something, but decided against it.

"Speak ya mind. It's not good to hold your tongue, that's how you get bad breath."

"Nothing, just watch him that's all."

I knew that wasn't what he was going to say, but I didn't want to further press the issue. When we arrived to my house, Ralph said a quick 'goodbye' and got in his car and left. I guess he was feeling some type of way.

Since I was without the kids, I decided to clean the house from top to bottom and rearrange a few things. Stripping down to my bra and undies, I tied my hair up in a bun, and blasted my new Usher CD.

Three hours later, my house was spotless. The smell of brown sugar and honey suckle gave the house a nice cozy feel. I went through the cabinets and made a grocery list, while pulling out some Salmon to cook for dinner. Sautéing my veggies and shrimp in a garlic and butter herb sauce, I placed the fish in the mixture and allowed it to cook.

I made a small pot of rice, and some green beans to go along with my meal. Waiting for everything to cook, I rolled me a fat blunt, and grabbed a strawberry daiquiri Seagram from the refrigerator.

I took a seat on the counter sparking up my blunt and taking tokes until my food was ready. Instantly, memories of Stacks began to flood my mind. It started from the first day I bumped into his car, from the day he asked me to be his girl, the first time we had sex, to our first argument.

I laughed out loud at how well he knew me and how he always knew what I was thinking before I even said anything. It was hard to live the life I was now forced to live without my soul mate.

Shaking the thoughts out of my head, I grabbed my food, placed it in on a tray, and watched Paid In Full while I enjoyed my meal. My mind briefly wandered off to Joey, so I decided to give him a call. It rung the first couple of times, but then he started sending me to his voicemail. Shrugging my shoulders, I sent him a text, and finished my dinner in peace.

Chapter 9
Ashley

"No, she didn't!" I said handing Loye a glass of wine.

"Yes, bitch she did, she came to me with a picture of Lala and asked me to transform her into the girl like I'm some damn magician."

"Nah. That bitch was on some crazy type shit for real though," I laughed and took a sip of my wine.

"Tell me about it, but when you hear from chick tell that hoe run me my money please."

"I haven't heard from her since Stacks died."

"Well I'mma have to Google all the crazy homes in this bitch cause I still want my money."

I doubled over in laughter while holding onto my abdomen. Loye's crazy ass was killing me. Ashley was an ok chick, but I didn't too much care for her. All I needed was for her to fuck up Lala's life and now that Stacks was dead, her life was already ruined. I could only imagine her pathetic ass struggling to raise twins by herself and that alone made me sleep well at night.

"Well, bitch I'm get going so that I could beat traffic. I don't know why yo ass decided to come live way out here in the country and shit, but that ain't none of my business. Kiss my god baby when he wakes up from his nap," Loye said brushing his long bond mane. He then gathered his things and left.

I had been calling my fiancé over and over for the past five hours, but was still getting no answer. I knew that he was back from his cop convention, so I couldn't understand why this nigga felt the need to play these type of games.

Originally, the purpose of me getting with Detective Armstrong was for him to help me take Stacks down. We both had our motives, he wanted to take down Miami's biggest King Pin so that he could be up for that lead detective position, and I just wanted to cause Lala hell. But when Stacks died, everything else did too and we'd been dating since.

I couldn't have asked for a better man. He was a great father to my son. He took me from the slums of the Pork 'N' Beans Projects to a nice two-story house in Westen. I was driving an Audi truck, and we wanted for nothing. Most importantly, I finally knew how it felt to have a guy really love you.

"Mama," Ashton cried out from his room.
"Mommy is coming baby."

I went to his room and lifted him up. Ruffling his head full of hair, I walked him over to my bed, so that I could change his diaper. Once I was done, I opened a bag of dehydrated apples and sat them in front of him with a cup of juice. I allowed the Sprout channel to steal his attention while I cleaned up and made dinner.

In the midst of stirring the soup, I took a whiff of the Curve for men cologne that I loved so much. A pair of strong hands wrapped around my hips, as a wet tongue glided across my neck causing my body to tremble in pleasure.

"Where have you been?" I asked trying my hardest not to moan.

"I went by my brother's club to talk to him for a bit," he said and slipped his hands in the waist of my shorts. "What's for dinner?"

"Chicken noodle soup and rice."

"What did I tell you about all that starch?"

"Well, how else are you supposed to eat chicken soup?" I asked and rolled my eyes. He was such a health freak, always watching my eating habits. It was cute at first, but now it was starting to become so fucking annoying.

"How about we eat the soup without rice, I'm pretty sure it's hearty enough."

"Whatever Joey."

He ripped my shirt off my body and pushed me up against the hallway wall. Putting one of my breasts in his mouth, he bit on it before sucking on it. I arched my back and pushed his head deeper into my breasts. I enjoyed the way his mouth was feeling on them. His hand then found its way in my honey pot. Using my wetness, he started flicking my clit with his thumb and forefinger.

He started to speed up the pace and I begged and pleaded for him not to stop. Feeling my body go through the sensational motions of a nearing orgasm, I opened my legs wider. He pinched my love button with so much force that the pain had me instantly leaking.

I was panting and out of breath trying to regroup when he flung me over his shoulder and carried me over to the sofa. He tried to take control, but I pushed his hands away and mounted him.

Pulling his shirt from over his head, I licked his sexy, ripped chest. I allowed my tongue to outline every single one of his eight pack, before heading down south. Unbuckling his pants, I released the beast and dove in head first. I rotated my tongue around his dick as I used all my jaw muscles attempting to suck the black off his dick.

He groaned and pushed my head further down into his crotch. Loosening my throat, I swallowed his dick as if I was taking a pain reliever. My pussy started to pulsate as I give him head better than Becky herself.

Gathering more spit in my mouth, I allowed it to coat his dick as I gave him sloppy toppy until he was busting loads down my throat. Sliding on his dick, he let out a light moan and grabbed my hips. It'd been a minute since I had some of daddy's good dick, so I was going to enjoy it to the fullest. I thought I was in full control of the ride until he started to raise my hips to match his thrust.

"Oh gaaaaaaaaaawd," I cried in out in pure pleasure as he began to fuck me hard.

"You like when I punish this pussy."

"Yesssssss daddy I love it!!"

He flipped me over in a sixty-nine position and ate me out until I was cumming, screaming, and begging for mercy all at the same time. Turning me over, he placed each of my legs on his shoulders and fucked me while he pulled on my hair. Good thing I was wearing my natural hair. Pushing my legs back further, he fucked me while making my kitty purr for mercy.

"Oh, shit I'm about to nut."

"Hold that shit, I want to nut with you," he demanded digging deeper in my honey pot. I was trying my best to follow his command, but it was as if my pussy had a mind of its on. A few pumps later and I was cumming all over the place.

"So you hard of hearing?" he asked and flipped me over. "Assume the position!"

I tooted my ass in the air as he murdered my cat. I was five seconds away from calling the animal shelter on his ass for animal cruelty.

"Now, you can come," he said playing with my clit as he pumped in and out of me. He didn't have to repeat himself because I was near my peak. He held onto my waist as we both came together.

"Next time when daddy speaks, you listen," he whispered to my pussy before planting soft kisses on it.

We laid on the couch for a few more minutes before showering and sitting at the table as a family to have dinner. At this point, I was really happy with how life was turning out and I was determined to kill the bitch my man was fucking with. I wasn't a dumb bitch. The way he came home and fucked me, I knew there had to be another bitch. I just hoped she was ready for the heat I was about to bring her way.

Chapter 10
Amanda

Stacks kept asking me questions that I was running out of lies to answer with. This was becoming harder than I thought. I wasn't expecting him to have such a full recovery; even the doctors were shocked at how well he was able to remember things.

To avoid him, I started leaving the house earlier and coming in later. I told him that I had a job at the hospital that was five miles away. I even went as far as to leaving the house wearing scrubs and shit. If I would have known my plan would fail so miserably, I would have just killed Lala like I originally wanted to.

"So, what you want to do?" Tazz asked me as we sat in my car trying to figure out how I was going to keep everything running smoothly.

"To be honest, I don't even know."

"Do you think he knows?"

"Nah. I think he's just getting restless since we're not in Miami and I'm not giving him a valid reason as to why."

"Why don't you just off ol' girl and go back to Miami?"

"It's not that easy. I would have to kill her best friend, Ralph, and everyone else who's closely associated with him."

"Damn."

Damn was right. I was now in a fucked up situation that I didn't know how to get out of. I grabbed the blunt from Tazz's hand and took a long pull; I held it in until my eyes began to water. The instant buzz felt good, so I decided to do it a few more times anticipating the high.

"Chill out ma this ain't no regular weed."

"Roll up another one," I replied finishing up this blunt.

My shift was scheduled to end in three hours. I could come up with some bullshit excuse telling him I had to pick up an extra shift and that would cover up for me coming home late. I didn't have to worry about him popping up or calling because he was home with the twins, he had no car, and I made sure not to leave any phones around. I didn't want to chance him remembering someone's number and blowing my cover.

We sat in the car and smoked some more until it was time for Tazz to leave. After I dropped him off to his car, I got me a small hotel room and a few bottles of Patron. Sitting on the dirty dingy ground, I felt myself having another panic attack.

I was finally supposed to live the life I wanted with the man I loved and it was all going down the drain. Drowning the bottle of Patron, I banged it against the tile floor until it shattered. Picking up a sharp peace of glass, I located an area on my thigh and began cutting.

The first slice hurt since it had been a while since I'd done it. But once I was able to get through the initial shock, my body began to ride the waves. With every slice I made into my skin, I could feel myself becoming relaxed. I made another slice and I was dancing on cloud nine. Laying with my head back as if I was in a drug coma, my tongue hung out the side of my mouth as I sat there with a blank expression on my face.

Wiping the blood off my thigh with the stained comforter, I held down some pressure on the cuts to stop the bleeding. Getting up and walking to the bathroom, I doused a washcloth with alcohol and began wiping my cuts clean. I discarded my clothes and lay on the musty smelling bed. I had no intentions on going home tonight, so this would have to do.

***

The following morning, I woke up with a horrible headache. Brushing my teeth, I washed my face and dressed myself in the cotton candy pink scrubs I brought along with me. After checking out of the hotel, I decided to stop by IHOP to buy some breakfast.

Once I arrived home, I sucked in a deep breath before walking in. The house was quiet as I placed my keys on the key ring that was located by the door. I began to panic as I walked though all of the rooms and was not able to locate Stacks or the girls. I was about to call 911, until I heard some voices and water splashing coming from the bathroom.

Through the crack of the door, I watched as Stacks gave the girls their bath. It was a sweet moment that warmed my heart. As he lathered their little bodies with the baby wash, he made small talk with them. As if the girls understood what he was saying, they would babble and giggle.

"Girl, your mother finally decided to come home," he said to the girls never turning around to acknowledge my presence. The way he said it had chills running up and down my spine.

"I had to work a double."

"Yeah, right."

"What's that suppose to mean?"

"It means this makes no fucking sense! You have access to all my fucking money and you're trying to tell me you have to break your back and work? Explain that shit to me LALA!" he yelled adding emphasis on "my name".

"How many times do I have to tell you that I had to up and leave every fucking thing?"

"So, you mean to tell me you have no access to my bank accounts? Or that my father would intentionally let me sit up here in this fucking hellhole while my girl struggles? Something ain't adding the fuck up!"

"I had to move fast, I thought you were dead. ALL I WAS TRYING TO DO WAS PROTECT MY FAMILY!" I cried. "And if that meant us going into hiding and broke while depending on my career to pay bills then so be it. I was willing to sacrifice all that shit in order for us to be together. It's not always about the money!"

"Man, get out of here with that shit. I'm trying to bond with my daughters, if they're even mine anyways."

"You know what, fuck you!"

"I been stop doing that after you tried to give me some bap shit."

His words stung me deep in the heart. At that moment, I wanted to grab a gun, shoot him, the twins, and then end my life. I took off running with blurry vision due to the tears that were building up in my eyes. I needed a release and I needed one fast.

Grabbing a knife, I snatched my keys off the key ring, and ran to my car. I pulled off and sped to the nearest secluded area. Tearing a whole in the pants of my scrubs, I used the knife to do what I knew how to do best.

Chapter 11
Ralph

I was trying to call the number that Stacks called me from to check on him to see if everything was good, but I was not getting a response. I couldn't wait until he came so he can nip that shit that Lala had going on with that nigga in the bud. I wasn't no hater, but something about the kid wasn't right. He smelt like he was a fucking pig.

I honked my horn again, waiting on my baby mama to bring my son out. She knew I was on my way; so I didn't know why she ain't have him ready. Pulling out my phone, I called to let her know I was outside, but she kept forwarding my calls. Pissed off, I got out my car and went to go knock on the door.

"What?!" Amber yelled as she snatched the door open.

"Is Jr. ready?"

"If he was he would have been out here waiting on you!"

"Amber, I ain't got time to play these games with you today man I just want to take my son and that's all."

"Do you have my money?" She smacked her lips, placing a hand filled with long, colorful, fake nails on her hips.

"I gave you fifteen hundred dollars last week, plus I bought you a house, paid all of your utilities, put groceries in the refrigerator, and bought Jr. a whole new wardrobe. WHAT MORE DO YOU FUCKING WANT!?"

"Well, I have to pay Jr. football registration fees and he needs tutoring."

Not wanting to argue with her basic ass, I reached in my pockets and handed her a stack of money not even counting it. She ran her fingers through the band and her face lit up like a kid on Christmas morning. Stuffing the money in her bra, she smiled and yelled for my son to finish packing his bags. I was sick of looking at her dumb ass, so I went to the car to wait on my son. I then texted Lisa to let her know that I was on my way over in an hour and to be ready.

"Hey dad!" Jr. said as soon as he opened the car door.

"What's up boy?"

"Nothing just tryna keep the ladies off me."

"What you know about the ladies?" I laughed.

"Man dad they be all on me at recess. I be having these chicks going ham for me."

"Oh, yeah?"

"Yeah, ya boy nice."

"Well, how them grades looking?"

"On point as always dad, I'm not tryna have moms on me."

"Good looking, check me out, we about to go pick up Riley then go pick up Lisa so we can chill."

"Ms. Lisa so cute."

"Yeah, but she off limits, so just chill."

"We'll see," he said before turning on the DVD player.

When we arrived at Laurie's house, I had no problem picking up my daughter. She was ready and waiting by the door like always. I went to the door to greet her mother and to made sure she was good on money.

"Daddy, where are my flowers?" Ry asked me as soon as I made it to the door.

"Aww, shit! I forgot. We'll go pick you up some."

"No, daddy you're supposed to bring me some flowers every time you come pick me up," she pouted.

"I know I won't forget anymore. Go get in the car, Jr. is in there. Let me talk to your mom for a little bit."

"You good?" I asked Laurie once Riley was in the car.

"Yes, Ralph, we're fine, but watch your mouth when you're speaking to our daughter."

"Yeah, my bad."

"When are you bringing her home?"

"You can just pick her up from school Monday afternoon."

"Ok, well, have a good time and tell Jr. I said hi."

"Iight."

That was what I loved about Laurie; it was always so peaceful between us. I bet if I would have came over there with Riley, Amber would have started a scene and I probably wouldn't have been able to get Jr. for the weekend. My phone beeped letting me know that I had a text, punching in my lock code, I swiped the text icon to read the message.

MY FUTURE: I'm ready, hurry up!

ME: Chill I'm on my way I had to go pick up the kids.

MY FUTURE: Ok, well I'm ready.

I put my phone back in my pocket and stopped at Rosey's Flower Shop. I got Riley some yellow and white daisies, and bought Lisa some blue and white roses. Jr.

surprised me when he bought Lisa a bouquet of roses then pulled out his wallet and paid for it on his own. I had to shake my head at his little ass.

"Thank you daddy," Riley smiled smelling the flowers.

"Anything for you princess."

When we got to Lisa's house, we got out the car and knocked on the door. She opened the door wearing a pink and grey Juicy Couture jogging suit, with a pair of pink and grey Jordan's on her feet.

"You look very pretty Ms. Lisa, these are for you," Jr. said handing her the roses he brought her.

"Thank you baby, you look real handsome yourself," she replied bending down and giving him a kiss. He blushed then turned around and gave me a thumbs up.

"Hey Ry."

"Hey, Lisa, I missed you."

"I missed you too doll. How have you been?"

"I've been doing great."

"That's good."

"Damn, I can't get no love?" I interrupted.

"Hey, Ralph," Lisa rolled her eyes

"Lose the attitude, here you go ma." I said handing her the flowers. "You done packing?"

"What am I packing for?"

"Weekend at my house."

"I ain't agree to that, Ralph."

"Please, Lisa, it'll be fun," Riley begged.

"Ok, let me go grab my bags."

"Yay!!" the kids cheered as Lisa rolled her eyes at me again. I watched her ass jiggle in them sweats and I made plans on getting me some of that tonight once the kids was asleep.

We spent the whole day at the mall shopping and watching movies, and then we ended up at the Dade County fair. I tested out my hoop skills trying to win my girls some teddy bears while Lisa rode every single roller coaster with the kids. I ended up winning them each big

Dalmatian dogs. It was getting real late, so we grabbed dinner to go and headed to my house.

"Go in your room and wash up for dinner," I directed the kids as soon as we walked inside the house. While the kids were taking their baths, Lisa and I were in the kitchen making the plates.

"Where am I sleeping tonight?" Lisa asked and grabbed the fruit Punch Twister juice and poured some in each of the cups.

"In the king's castle," I answered as I sat down and ate my food.

"I ain't sleeping on that bed you been fucking that bitch on," she replied and took a seat across from me.

"You the only bitch I'mma be fucking in that bed."

"Oh, I got you bitch," she said throwing her cup of juice in my face. That's what I loved about her thug ass, she ain't take shit from no nigga and that shit was sexy as fuck.

The kids were back so we sat at the table and ate dinner like a family. It felt good to have my kids and the woman that I loved in my presence. It was time that I quit playing and make Lisa my wife, hell I might even put a baby in her ass just to keep that pussy on lock.

When we finished dinner, Lisa popped some popcorn and we sat in the family room watching scary movies. After the second movie, the kids were fast asleep, so I carried them to their rooms. Turning off the TV, then cleaning up the room, I headed upstairs where I heard the shower running.

Lisa was in the shower attempting to sing K. Michelle's *VSOP* when I walked in. Taking my clothes off, I pulled the door back and got in the shower with her.

"What the fuck you doing?" she asked and hit me with the sponge.

"I came to take a shower."

"You have five fucking bathrooms!"

"Ever heard of saving water," I said pushing her up against the shower wall. I covered her lips with mine so that she couldn't protest. Lifting her legs, I wrapped them around my waist and used my dick to play with her clit.

I could feel the vibrations of her moans coming from her throat as I continued to assault her tongue with my mouth. Even though we were in the shower, I could still feel the warmth of her wetness dripping down my legs. Her pussy was so hot that it was begging me to put it out of its misery. I rubbed on my dick until it was so hard that the veins began to appear.

Shoving my dick in her pussy, I held it there. It had been a minute since I been in her pussy and I forgot how good it was. She started rotating her hips and grinding on me causing me to bitch up a little bit. I held her up against the wall by her waist and started deep stroking her pussy. I knew she was missing the kid by the way her pussy was crying out in pleasure. I still held her tongue captive in my mouth while she hummed for mercy.

I felt her pussy start to contract around my dick, so I pumped harder and faster. I freed myself from her lips so that I could grab one of her breasts in my mouth.

"Oh fuuuuuuuuk!" she moaned when I bit down hard on her shoulder blade causing her to shutter.

"Oh, shit don't stop," she demanded. "Beat this pusssssssssssy up!!!"

I was really good at following directions, so I kept fucking her until she creamed all over my wood. Lifting her above my head, I used my mouth to suck her dry. She started grinding on my mouth, so I bit her clit and latched onto it, sucking until she cursed me. I rolled my tongue over her now swollen pearl before using it to bring her to another nut. She collapsed in my arms, so I adjusted the showerhead so that I could rinse her body off. Stepping out of the shower, I grabbed a towel and dried her body off.

Laying her on my bed, I wasn't done with her ass yet. I quickly went to go check on the kids and made sure that they were still asleep before closing my bedroom door.

I grabbed the pineapple, edible body oil and rubbed her down with it before licking it clean off her body. That alone had her already busting her third nut. Flipping her over, I fucked her until she lost her voice then fell asleep.

Chapter 12

Lala

Temperature's rising

And your body's yearnin' for me

So, come here baby

Girl, lay it on me

I place no one above thee

Oh, take me to your ecstasy

It seems like you're ready

(Seems like you're ready)

Seems like you're ready

(Girl, are you ready)

To go all the way, all the way.....

R. Kelly's voice sweetly sung through my stereo system as I slowly grinded in front of the mirror. I was getting ready for my date with Joey and if he played his cards right, tonight could be the night. Slipping on my sexy black lace Victoria's Secret thong set, I sexily propped my legs and gently rubbed my body down with body butter while still grinding to the music.

I fingered the many different scents that I had on my vanity and decided that my *Heat* by Beyoncé perfume was perfect. After spraying down the sexual parts of my body, I slipped my body in the white, silk Donna Karen wrap around dress that I just purchased.

The two slits on the sides came up to my mid thigh showing of my sexy, smooth toned legs. I rubbed on the tattoo I had on my leg and for a minute guilt started to settle in. I had to remind myself that Stacks was dead and that it was ok for me to move on.

Taking the large flexi rods out of my hair, I fingered my curls and allowed them to loosely drop down my back. The gate bell started to ring and I hit the button on the wall. I saw the guards checking Joey before letting him in. I was kind of hesitant on letting him come pick me up at my house, so I decided that I would meet him at the guesthouse that was around back from my house.

My mansion was so big that it looked like a whole bunches house scattered around. Since the death of Stacks, I used remodeling as a way to cope and I was glad I did because unless I knew you personally, you wasn't able to tell which house I actually lived in.

I sent the guard a message to let him in the guesthouse and to keep a close eye on him until I came over. Although I felt that Joey was harmless, I still wanted to take what Ralph said into consideration. Checking my handbag, I made sure I had everything including my handgun.

Life of a Queen Pin taught me to always stay strap. Taking the secret elevator that I had hidden behind a bookcase, I made my way to the back where the guesthouse was located. Giving the guard a head nod, I entered from the back door and appeared as if I had been in the house the whole time.

"Sorry to keep you waiting."

"It was no trouble at all," he said and then licked his lips. "You look beautiful."

"Thank you," I blushed.

"Are you ready to go?"

"Yes."

"Where are we going?" I asked as I strapped the seatbelt across my chest once I got into the car.

"To a nice little spot I think you're going to like."

A few minutes later, we arrived at Romeo's Café. I knew he had to be getting mad bread from his clubs because this place wasn't cheap. Stacks took me here all the time; it was actually one of my favorite places to eat. We were regulars and the whole staff knew us by name. We would practically walk in and was catered to. By the end of the night our meal would usually total $568.00 plus the generous three hundred dollars tip Stacks always left our host. I was praying Joey knew what type of place this was and wasn't depending on me to go half on the bill with him.

"How are you, Lala?" Jack greeted me as soon as we walked in

"I'm good Jack, how's Sally and the kids?"

"They're great?" he looked down at my tummy and noticed it was flat. "And the baby?"

"Babies," I corrected. "They're fine, I actually had twins."

"Twins?" he gasped.

"Yes. Baby B was hiding behind Baby A the whole time."

"What a blessing," he said and grabbed two menus. "The usual table?" he asked looking Joey over.

"No, I actually made us reservations," Joey answered. "Under Armstrong."

"Ok, here we go. You sure you don't want the usual table?"

"No, Jack that's fine," Joey snarled.

The table Joey was able to get was not as lavish as the table Stacks and I always sat at, but I wasn't complaining. I really didn't want to sit at a table I used to enjoy intimate dinners at with my deceased fiancé.

"You've been here before?" Joey asked as we were seated.

"Yes a few times."

"Welcome to Romeo's- wait, Lala, darling is that you?" the waitress asked.

"Yes GiGi," I smiled hoping she would just take our orders and go about her business.

"Will you be having the usual?"

"Yes," I replied, if he couldn't afford it, I was prepared to pay for it myself.

"Would you like the usual Sta- I mean new guy?" GiGi stuttered when she realized that I wasn't with Stacks.

"No. But I'll have the Wagyu Fillet Mignon, roasted garlic potatoes, with the sour cream and chives sauce, and the bacon seared asparagus. By the way it's Joey, GiGi," he replied and handed her the menu. "Also a bottle of your finest wine."

"So, Ms. Lala, I had no idea you were so famous?"

"What do you mean?" I asked taking a sip of my water.

"The who restaurant is practically calling you by your name."

"I guess because I've dined here before," I shrugged.

"What do you do for a living, if you don't mind me asking?" he asked trying to get personal.

"I am a doctor that owns three clinics," I lightly fibbed; it wasn't his business anyways.

"Really?"

"Yes really."

"Well that explains why you're so well known," he said throwing some shade. I was going to reply, but GiGi returned with the food.

Dinner was eaten in silence. The tension in the air was so thick that I could cut it with my steak knife. Joey called for the bill after dessert and I was anxious to see how this was going to play out. He pulled out his black card and handed it to GiGi without even checking the price. He then pulled out a three hundred dollar tip and put it on the table. Something about that gesture had me feeling some type of way, but I just shrugged it off.

"I'm sorry if I offended you." He apologized as he led me to the dimly lit sitting area.

"No offense taken."

"May I have this dance?" he asked as he reached his hands out to me.

I allowed him the swoop me into his arms as we slow danced to the beat. He used his big strong hands to caress my back before resting them on my ass. He pulled me in closer; the coolness from the mint he ate tickled my neck as he whispered his desires for me.

I was so lost in a trance that if he unwrapped my dress in front of all these people and decided to have his way with me, I was willing to allow him to. I moaned as he bit on my neck and started gently nibbling on it.

"You ready to go?" he groaned.

"Yessss."

The ride to our destination was a blissful one. He had his hands up my dress playing in my treasure the whole drive that I was on my third orgasm when we finally arrived to our stop. I was still skating on cloud nine that I didn't even realize that we were at his house. He lifted me and carried me into the house and to his bedroom. He laid me down on the plush Nautica sheet set that decorated the bed, and then left the room.

My pussy began to jump in excitement when he returned with a bowl of chocolate and a plate of strawberries. He stripped my body until I resembled the day I entered this world. Rubbing his hand over my perfectly waxed pussy, he dipped his finger in the bowl of chocolate and coated my pussy lips with it. My body waited in anticipation as I waited for him to lick it all of.

"Sssssssss," I hissed as he used his tongue to torture me. He picked up a strawberry with his teeth, dipped it in the chocolate and used it to play with my love button. I spread my legs wider and allowed the fresh fruit to bring me to another orgasm. With that bowl of chocolate and strawberries, he brought me to ecstasy multiple times. Cleaning me up with his tongue, he shoved it in my mouth so that I could taste the sweetness from the chocolate and my juice. I sucked on his tongue savoring every drop.

"You ready for me?" he asked in a deep husky voice

Unable to speak, all I did was nod my head. Grabbing a condom from his dresser, he applied it to his dick. He wasn't as big as Stacks, but he wasn't disappointing either. With one gentle thrust, he entered a spot that was supposed to belong to Stacks. I was starting to feel guilty for giving myself away, but with every stroke he made, my pussy melted and every ounce of guilt I had was gone.

Leaving Passion marks all over my neck, he made sweet love to me that it scared me. He wasn't rough; he was gentle as he caressed my skin, paying attention to everything that brought me pleasure. He studied my moans and continued to stroke in that direction until he found my G-spot.

"Fuuuuuuuuk!" I cried as he sped up and unmercifully nailed my spot. He squeezed on my breast and shoved them in his mouth as if he was starving and I was his only source of food. He started to fuck me until my vision went blurry and for a second I thought I was legally blind.

He held my legs down as they began to tremble and forced me to ride the wave of my now sixth orgasm. Moments later, I felt his dick grow harder, I matched his every trust until the Magnum he wore captured all of his seeds. Exhaustion took over us as we fell asleep all sweaty and sticky.

***

The next morning, I woke up to the smell of maple bacon. Stretching I noticed the tray of food that sat in front of me.

"Good morning beautiful," Joey greeted me.

"Good morning," I smiled.

"Eat up your breakfast, I left something for you in the bathroom, so you can shower when you're done. I'll be down in the gym if you need me," he winked before walking out of the room.

Picking up my phone, I checked for any missed calls and text messages. I had a multimedia message from Anna; it was a picture of the twins with Mickey and Minnie. I was missing my kids something terrible and was glad that they would be coming home in two weeks. Finishing up my breakfast, I walked to the bathroom and handled my hygiene. Dressed in the shorts and t-shirt Joey left me, I slid my feet in the loafers and went down to the gym.

I could hear Joey in a heated conversation with someone and before I could get close enough to listen in, he signaled for me to hold on and stepped outside. I tried my best to eavesdrop, but it was as if he was whispering. Sitting on the workout bench, I pulled out my phone and made a lunch date with Lisa.

"Sorry about that, work."

"It's ok," I said and stood up. "Thanks for the clothes they fit perfectly."

"You're welcome. Let me go freshen up for work then I'll drop you home."

"Ok. Cool."

Forty-five minutes later, he was dressed in some black slacks with a blue button down shirt, and black loafers. The Tommy Hilfiger cologne he was wearing brought back memories of James and I instantly felt sick to my stomach. He decided to switch up his cars because now we were riding in his Camaro; I guess he was getting paper after all.

"I had a really great time with you," he said pulling up to my guesthouse

"Likewise," I replied.

He walked me to the door where we shared a nice, long kiss.

"I'll call you later," he said breaking our kiss.

"I'll be waiting," I blushed.

I watched him drive away then, walked over to my house. Punching the code in the door, I was greeted by the smell of the French vanilla Glad spray that I hung in the foyer. I sat at my desk and reviewed the tapes of the house activities that occurred while I was gone. I trusted my guards, but you couldn't be too sure. Everything looked as if it was in order, so I went upstairs and changed into some jeans and a Juicy Couture crop top.

The loafers matched what I was wearing, so I decided to leave them on. I texted Lisa to let her know that I was on my way over. Punching in the key code to my garage, I browsed my selections before I decided on pushing my Lamborghini.

Shoulders sideways, smack it, smack it in the air
Legs movin' side to side, smack it in the air
Legs movin' side to side, smack you in the air
Shoulders sideways, smack it, smack it in the air
Smack it, smack it in the air
Legs movin' side to side, smack it, smack it in the air
Smack it, smack it in the air

Wave your hands side to side, put it in the air
Wave your hands side to side, put it in the air
Clap, clap, clap like you don't care
Smack that, clap, clap, clap like you don't care
(I know you care)

I was jamming to Beyoncé's new song *7/11* when I pulled up to a red light. Something told me to look over to my right, so I turned around and was starring in the eyes of the devil. My body was instantly filled with rage as I watched him bob his head to his music in his drop top like he wasn't a wanted man.

Even though Stacks was dead, I still made it my business to deal with his ass once I was ever able to catch up with him and today was my lucky day. Plus, part of me strongly believed that he had something to do with Stacks' death.

The light turned green, so I turned on my signal, and turned in the lane behind him. I snapped a picture of his license plate and allowed two cars to get in front of me, so that it wouldn't look obvious that I was tailing him. He turned into a parking lot of a hotel.

I snapped a picture of him as he got out his car and headed inside of the lobby. Locating Ralph's name in my contact list, I hit the green call button and put the phone to my ear.

"Columbiana, what's good?"

"Shut up," I laughed. "But on a real note, guess who I found?"

"Stacks?" he hesitantly asked, it was something about the way he asked that, which made me feel like he knew something I didn't know.

"Stacks?! Be for real man!"

"Uh- then who?"

"Bear."

"Bear?!"

"Yes. Bear! I followed him to the hotel."

"Where he at?"

"He went inside one of the rooms, but I'm looking right at the back of his car, so I'll be able to keep an eye on him."

"Text me the location, I'm coming," he said and then hung up the phone. I sent him a text of where I was and sat back and waited for him to come.

I was engrossed in my thoughts that I didn't hear the tapping on my window. Unlocking the door, I let Ralph in.

"Any movements on him?"

"Nah. He still in the room."

"Where his car?"

"Right there," I said pointing to the car that was parked by the lobby.

"Iight go chill with ya girl I got this."

"I want in."

"I got you ma'. I'mma get up with you when we got him at the chop shop."

"Ok."

Ralph got out of the car and walked inside of the lobby. I spotted a few of my workers in an Expedition beside me, I hit them with a head nod that meant handle business before pulling off. I replayed Beyoncé's *7/11* and bopped to the beat. I was finally getting some type of justice for Stacks and it felt good.

Chapter 13

Ralph

I sat back and rolled a joint with my crew waiting on Bear's ass to show face. I was happy as fuck that I was able to get up with that nigga and even happier because Stacks was going to enjoy killing the fat bitch. Speaking of Stacks, I did not know how he was going to take Lala fucking the next nigga. I wasn't dumb, I saw the hickeys and bite marks that decorated her neck and chest. I just hoped he understood the circumstances and shit ain't get too crazy.

"That's that nigga right there," I said to my crew once I spotted him getting inside his car with a white chick on his arm.

"What's the plan boss?" one of my workers asked.

"We gon' follow his ass until we can snatch him up." I put the blunt to my lips and took a long pull.

Bear's ass took us on a long ride through Miami until he finally pulled over at a gas station. When he went in to pay for the gas, I hopped out and went to go holla at ol' girl that was in the car with him

"Yo' ma you want to make a quick three thousand dollars?" I asked keeping my eye on the gas station door.

"Yes! How?"

"All you have to do is lead the dude you came with to a secluded location, so that I could have a quick word with him."

"You're not going to hurt him are you?"

"No, he's actually my brother and I've been having a hard time trying to get in contact with him."

"Ok. He's going to drop me off at home. I'll just invite him in and you two can talk."

"Cool, but one thing, don't tell him that we spoke or he won't agree to speak with me. Here's half of the money. I'll give you the other half when the job is complete," I said handing her some money and jogging back to the car. I made it just in time because as soon as I closed my door, he was walking out. I watched him pump the gas, then pull off. I waited a few minutes before following him.

We ended up in the projects and I was confused because I thought the chick said he was bringing her home. At first, I thought it was a set-up until I seen both of them exit the car and her unlocking the front door. A few minutes later, she came outside in search for me, I honked my horn then waved her over.

"He's in my bedroom, you're more than welcome to go talk to him."

"Is this your spot?" I asked eyeing her. She looked like a well together white girl that didn't belong in the jects.

"Yes."

"Lead the way," I said following behind her, I signaled for the crew to follow behind me.

The inside of the house looked way better than the outside. I left the door open and pulled out my gun motioning for the girl to be quiet. I walked to the bedroom where I heard him talking on the phone. His back was facing towards me; I put my gun to the dome of his head and waited for him to turn around.

"Snakes eventually get caught," I said staring him in the eyes. I could feel the fear radiating off of his body, but he wanted to pretend like he wasn't fazed.

"Pull the trigger nigga," he taunted.

"Nah. I'mma let Stacks do it?"

"Well, go dig his ass up then," he laughed.

"Laugh now cry later nigga, Stacks ain't dead!"

His eyes became wide as saucers as he realized he was screwed. Not wanting to waste any more time with his big ass, I hit him twice in the head with the butt of my gun that knocked him out cold. I let his body drop to the floor like a sack of potatoes and called out to my crew to come carry him to the car.

"I thought you said you wasn't going to hurt him."

"I lied," I shrugged screwing on the silencer on my gun. Before she could say another word, I put two in her dome. I knew she was innocent, but I ain't want to risk her going to the police. I spent five years behind bars, and it'll be a cold day in hell before I go back.

I sent Lala a text letting her know to meet me at the spot. When we got there, I had my men tie his fat ass to a chair. I wanted to have some fun with him, so I decided to use his ass as a punching bag. I owed him an ass whooping anyways for being so disloyal.

With every punch I swung, I heard something either crack or felt blood splatter all over my body. Blow after blow his head rocked back and forth as teeth started to fly out of his mouth. I had to compose myself, no matter how badly I wanted to kill him, I was going to save his life for Stacks.

The doors to the spot opened and Lala followed by Lisa walked in. I knew Lisa had some bad blood with Bear, so I didn't trip when I saw her dressed in all black, wearing a pair of tims and a pair of diamond platted brass knuckles.

WHAP! WHAP! WHAP! WHAP!

Was all that could be heard as Lala and Lisa took turns beating on him. I watched the assault in amazement before deciding to break it up.

"Chill ladies y'all gon' kill him."

"That's the plan, right?"

"Yeah, but I ain't want to take him out so easy. I'mma fuck with his ass for a little bit. I want this nigga to beg for death."

"I guess, let's go shopping," Lala said upper-cutting Bear one good time that knocked him and the chair over.

"I need a refill too," Lisa said kicking Bear in the head with her boots. They both walked out of the warehouse, holding a conversation about their plans for the rest of the day.

"Them so gangster ass bitches," I chuckled, taking my ringing phone out of my pockets.

"Yo."

"Come get me. I'm sending you the address now," Stacks said before he disconnected the call.

Chapter 14

Stacks

Grabbing some suitcases that I found in the closet, I packed as much of the twins' things that could fit. I gave them each a bath and bathed them before strapping them in their stroller. I pulled my fitted cap over my head so that the brim was covering my eyes.

Pulling the hoody over my head, I pulled the strings tight in attempt to hide my identity. I was trying to reach my destination and back before that snake bitch Amanda came back from her so called job.

I pushed them until I was able to locate a nearby Catholic church. Placing them in front of the church's doors, I put the bags next to them and rung the bell. I waited off to the side until one of the nuns came out. She looked around before bending down and taking the babies and bringing them inside with her. As soon as the church doors closed and I was sure that the girls were safe, I jogged back to the house and waited for the evil conniving bitch.

I had my suspicions about her from day one, but I needed to get to the bottom of this shit. With the DNA test proving that those little girls weren't mine, I could carry out my plan with a peace of mind. Although I knew the kids weren't mine, I wouldn't be able to sleep well at night with just a gut feeling, I needed to know for sure. After hitting the send button on the text that I was sending Ralph, I sat and waited.

The sound of the door being unlocked woke me op out of my catnap. I faked sleep and watched out of the corner of my eyes as Amanda walked through the house. I felt her presence in the room for a brief moment, and then she walked in the twins' room in search from them. When she realized that they weren't in their beds, I heard her footsteps stomp around the house in a frantic search for them.

"Stacks!" she shouted, shaking me out of my sleep.

"What?" I yawned, faking as if I was just waking up.

"Where are the girls?"

"What girls?"

"Our daughters!!"

"Those wasn't my daughters, but the twins are at the church."

"What the fuck are you talking about?"

"This," I said handing her the DNA results. She began to fidget as she read the words on the page

"Who you working with Amanda?"

"Wh-h-h-at are you talking about?"

"Stop playing dumb, I know who the fuck you are so speak before I kill yo ass," I said revealing the gun I was able to cop from the dude on the corner. She started to shake and tremble in fear as I pulled the trigger.

"You promise you won't kill me if I tell you?"

"Yes," I lied "Now, get to talking."

"My cousin Tazz was working for Bear, they had plans to kill you, but I staged it, so that I could spare your life."

"So, you was working with that nigga Bear all along?"

"No."

"Where is Bear?"

"I don't know!"

"Wrong answer bitch!"

POW! POW! POW!

Her body hit the ground and she began to try and slowly crawl away. Standing above her, I shot her three times in the back putting her out of her misery. I went out back and cut all the gas lines. Once I was satisfied with my work, I left the house. I made it to a diner where I sat and waited for Ralph to come.

An old school Chevy Caprice that pulled in the parking lot playing loud music caught my attention. When I noticed it was my nigga Ralph, I got up and walked outside.

"This how we do it now?" I asked walking up on him.

"My nigga, my nigga!" he replied embracing me. We stood in a brotherly embrace for a few more minutes before breaking apart

"Damn I can't believe it's you."

"Well believe it baby!" I said leaning against his car "This shit clean though!"

"Yeah, I know, but my collection got nothing on Lala, she got a whole garage built."

"Word?"

"Yeah, she been doing the damn thing since you been gone."

"What you mean?" I asked getting in the car. I prayed that he wasn't finna tell me that Lala done moved on with no square ass nigga and had him raising my kids.

"She took over."

"Took over what?"

"Your position, your father stepped down and now she is the connect."

"What the fuck you mean?!" I began to flame, she was supposed to be home raising my kids not out in the streets of Miami being a fucking Queen Pin.

"Exactly what I said nigga! She running the fucking show."

"Who authorized that shit? And what the fuck is your position?"

"Your pops. I'm just her right hand, just like I was yours."

"I need to go to Columbia," I said, pissed that my father would put my girl in that position.

"You don't want to go home first?"

"Nah, I'll deal with her ass later. How are my kids?"

"They're good, big as hell. You got a son Amire and a daughter Amiracle."

"They look like me?" I asked smiling.

"Amire is a mini Stacks, that lil nigga looks just like you."

"So, how Lala been?"

"At first, she was depressed as hell but she got better with time. She own three clinics, too."

"You mean to tell me my bitch running the streets of Miami and clinics?"

"Yeah. That's her way of making her money look legal. Ya' girl real smart."

"I see," I smiled. "Ralph, I'mma ask you something and keep it one hundred with me."

"No, doubt son, I'm always real about mine."

"Is Lala fucking with another nigga?" I asked, afraid to know the answer. He gave me a look that answered my question. I felt my heart break, and my anger rise. I had to remind myself that she thought I was dead.

"Who is he?" I asked.

"Some square ass nigga. Something about his ass don't sit well with me though."

"What you mean?"

"I just get this bad vibe from kid, like he a pig or something."

"Damn. I'mma have to handle that. Yo' when you get to that exit see if you can find a mall, I ain't tryna shop in Miami." I really didn't want to risk running into Lala, so I just figured I'll just get what I need here then just hop on my private plane and head to Columbia.

"You got me bra? I'll pay you back when I get to the crib," I asked as we pulled into the mall

"You ain't even got to worry about it nigga, I gotchu."

We went in the mall and shut shit down. I didn't want to over do it since Ralph told me that Lala never got rid of my things. I just copped the new Jordan's that were released while I was *dead*, a few suits, watches, and other things that I would be needing on my trip. After dropping eight racks at the mall, I made Ralph take me to a hotel, so that I could shower and get fresh.

I took a nice shit, showered, than shaved and got dressed. I wore a three-piece tan Armani suit, with a white button down shirt underneath it. I matched it with a pair of tan Armani loafers, a gold diamond dial Michael Kors watch, with a pair of gold diamond studs. Spraying myself with the Armani Code cologne, I checked myself out in the mirror. I was looking on point, but my haircut was a little off, so before our drive to the Miami airport, I had Ralph stop by a Barber to freshen my haircut up.

The long drive was completed and I was finally at the airport boarding my private plane. I noticed that there was another plane parked in my reserved area and Ralph informed me that it was Lala's. I guess my baby was doing big things. The long drive had a nigga worn out, so as soon as the plane took off I was out cold.

***

"Nigga get up, we here." Ralph shook me as we landed. The driver that usually took us back and forth looked at me as if he'd seen a ghost. I had to laugh because he kept saying "Senor Stacks" as if I was an imposer. Arriving to the mansion, I began to get a little nervous. I just hoped my father didn't catch a heart attack when he saw me.

"Papa," I yelled through the house as soon as the maid let me in. She was new, so she really didn't know that I was Lazarus.

"Dios mío! (Oh my God!)," my dad yelled seeing me. He immediately ran over to me and started to touch my face making sure that I was actually alive and that it was me. He reached for my wrist and turned it over. I had a distinctive birthmark there that only both of us shared. When he was able to local the birthmark, he broke down in my arms crying.

"Shhhh, it's ok, Papa, I'm here."

"Oh, my son!"

"Yes, Papa."

"This is incredible, but tell me what happened because I sat front row at your funeral and watched you get buried." We sat at the table where I told him and Ralph the events on what took place leading me here.

"Enough about me, Papa, I hear that you have Lala running things."

"Yes, that is true."

"Why? Ralph was next in line."

"With all due respect, Ralph, I just wanted to keep it in the family. When I realized that you had a son, I decided to pass it down to Lala in hopes of it getting passed down to your son."

"But she's is a mother," I interjected.

"She is and a very good one. Lala is a very strong woman. She picked up where you left off and the family business have not suffered because of it, well except of the Carla situation."

"What Carla situation?"

"Apparently, Carla was stealing money and drugs from us, but Lala handled it?"

"Handled it how?" I asked as my heart began to beat rapidly, I didn't want any wars starting especially since I had two kids.

"We cut them off."

"Do you think that was wise?"

"Yes, because now money has been tripling." I sat back and took in everything my pops had to say. It was all making sense and I was actually proud of Lala.

We went over more business proposals and I was really impressed. Ralph decided to go home the following day and I decided to stay in Columbia for a few more days. It was not like I didn't want to go home, I was just afraid to. I didn't know what to expect from Lala with all these changes and I also didn't know how I was going to take her seeing someone else. Plus, I wanted to go see Carla and hear her side of the story first.

Chapter 15
Ashley

I was laying in the sheets that Joey and I had just finished making sweet love in smiling from ear to ear. I was so deep in love with this man and I was so ready to spend the rest of my life with him. I heard the shower turn on, and the smell of his Adidas body wash filled the room. My legs was still sore from the hurting he put on my pussy that I didn't even want to move, so I decided to wait in bed for him to return.

After his shower, I watched him as he dressed in a Nike jogging suit, and lace up a pair of matching Nikes.

"Where are you going?" I asked watching him pull out a bag to pack.

"I have a case to work on, I'm going to work from the station with my partner."

"Why would you work from a police station when you can work from that big ass office you got in the back!" I yelled.

"Lower your voice before you wake up my son!"

"You fucking another bitch?" I asked as I got out of the bed.

"I don't have time for this shit."

"Make time then." I was now in his face with titties bouncing and all.

"Why are you being so insecure?"

"Because you're giving me every reason to be! You stay out late, disappear for days, are you living a double life?"

"No, I'm working! You knew how demanding my job was when we met, so why are you giving me grief now?"

"I'm pregnant," I whispered.

"Come again."

"I"M PREGNANT!" I cried. I loved Joey with all of my heart, but I wasn't ready for another baby yet.

"Ahh shit!"

"Excuse me?"

"I mean do you think this is a right time to have another baby?"

"What are you trying to say?"

"I'm not saying anything, I'm asking you, do you think it is a right time to have another baby?"

At that very moment I broke down crying. This confirmed all of my suspicions; he in fact was living a double life. I kicked myself for falling in love with yet another jackass. I cried because I couldn't catch a break, I wasn't going to amount to anything but being a side bitch.

"Shhhhh don't cry. I have to get going, but we will finish up this conversation later," he said and kissed me on the lips before walking to the bathroom. I quickly grabbed my robe and threw it on. I walked outside to his car and enabled the GPS application I had installed in his car.

"What are you doing outside naked?"

"I'm not naked, I have on a robe. I thought I heard the alarm on the cars go off."

"Ok. Well I'll call you when I get to the station." I watched him get inside his car and drive off.

I went in the house and grabbed my iPad. Turning on the GPS, I was able to track Joey. I watched as he stopped at a Burger King, then he was heading in the direction of the police station. I sat and watched his car until he finally came to a complete stop. I was relieved when I saw the little dot on the screen stop at the police station indicating that he was telling the truth. Maybe I was overreacting. Putting my iPad down, I sent Joey a cute "I love you text." and prepared breakfast for my son and I.

I still wasn't sure what I was going to do with the baby that was growing in me. Although, I was not ready to be a mother again, I couldn't imagine life without my son so an abortion was out of the question. Looking down at my engagement ring, I figured since we was going to be married anyways that maybe having another baby wouldn't be so bad after all. I was just hoping that we were on the same page.

Chapter 16

Joey

"Detective Armstrong, how's the case coming along?" My boss asked me snapping me out of my thoughts.

"Everything is going great."

"Don't let me down, I fought for you when the mayor's office wanted this case closed after the death of Stacks. I'm funding your investigation, so if you don't nail this one on the head that's your ass."

"I understand, Sir, I won't let you down," I assured the chief who was also my father.

My father had been on the force for over thirty years. He was ranked number one in the city of Miami and there wasn't a case that he couldn't solve. He rightfully earned his position, and all the respect that came along with it.

To him, I was another failure. I was forty-two and only still ranked a detective. He often compared me to my brother Jimmy who was a retired vet from the army. I was determined to make my father proud; I was no longer going to live in my brother's shadow.

"Did you get any information on, Lisa," he asked.

"Dad, her name is Lala."

"You address me as Sir, and I know her name is Lala, but I am inquiring about her friend Lisa. Have you gotten any information on her?"

"Why would I need information on Lisa if it's Lala running the cartel?"

"You stupid idiot! This is why you will never be shit. Lisa and Lala are close friends; Lisa is your link to Lala. I hope you didn't think sticking your little dick in Lala was going to solve this damn case!" he spat.

"I'll get right on it Sir."

"Piece of shit, is so worthless," he ranted while walking out of the office.

Hitting the spacebar on my computer, I ran Lisa's name through our database. She came up in our system with having a gun charge two years ago. I put in a request to have a family background check done on her. Picking up my phone, I texted Lala and invited her to join me for dinner.

I wasn't a fool; I knew Lala didn't get all of her money from her clinics. I've visited them and although they look like very successful establishments, it wasn't enough to have her living like the first lady. My phone buzzed and it was a text from Ashley asking me if I needed her to bring me dinner. I quickly declined and told her my father made dinner plans for us.

At first, my relationship with Ashley was strictly business. She needed me and I needed her. She wanted me to take down Stacks and I wanted to because bringing down a king pin of Stacks status would bring me a lot of recognition. In the midst of everything, I fell in love with her and her son, which I adopted as my own. She had no clue that I was still working on this case.

I was there at the funeral the day that they buried Stacks. I also followed my gut feeling that told me to keep tabs on Lala. At first all she did was stay home. Then suddenly she started making the frequent trips to Columbia. I figured she was going to visit Stacks' father, but not once did she ever bring one of her kids with her, which led me to believe that those visits were business meetings.

The thought of Lala taking over the cartel kept running through my mind until I decided to bring it to my father's attention. My first time coming to him, he laughed in my face as if I was some lame joke. But once I was able to get some information on her from someone that we arrested for selling drugs to a decoy, my father decided to give me a chance.

The mayor, however, didn't budge and decided that he wasn't going to fund our operation. My father knew how big cracking a case like this was, so he allowed me to work it funding it on his own.

Lala sent me a text me back agreeing to my plans and informing that she would be driving her car. I was really hoping that she was going to allow me to come pick her up because I had some new bugs that the tech guy delivered to me that I wanted to plant in her house.

I needed to know the times and locations of the drop in order to bring her in custody. I had enough information on her to arrest her, but with the type of money she was bringing in she would be able to afford an attorney that could have the case thrown out. I needed something that was going to stick.

Wrapping up my paper work for the day, I headed over to my house. Even though I had a family house that I shared with Ashley, I decided to still keep my house and I was glad that I did. Browsing through the fridge, I searched for something that I could use to make a quick meal. Pulling out some chicken breast, I put them under hot, running water so that they could thaw out. I then grabbed a few packs of mash potatoes and a bag of green beans.

Preparing our meal, I put everything on low and headed towards the shower. My phone started ringing, and when I checked the screen, I saw it was Ashley, so I ignored her call and proceeded with getting ready. Thirty minutes later, I was refreshed and dressed to impress. The True Religion cargos and shirt that I wore were neatly pressed, and the fresh out of the box pair of J. Crew Boats that were on my feet matched my outfit perfectly.

Filling the vase with warm water, I dropped a crushed Tylenol pill, a trick I learned from my mother, in the water and placed the fresh roses that I brought in it. I then set the table for two adding two long candles in the middle of the table.

The scent of the rosemary-baked chicken breast took over the house as I placed them on a platter and sat it on the table. I warmed the rolls in the oven and grabbed the butter out of the fridge. I was putting the final touches on dinner when the doorbell rang.

"Hey you look nice." I greeted Lala who was standing in front of me in a black mesh mini dress that displayed her every curve. My mouth began to water at the thought of tasting her juicy pussy again. Even if I had no intentions on being romantically involved with Lala, that didn't mean I couldn't have my cake and eat it too.

"Thanks, you smell delicious," she winked and walked inside the house. As I was closing the door behind her, I could have sworn that I seen someone in a car in front of my house. Thinking it was paranoia; I shook it off and closed the door.

"What's for dinner?" Lala asked and took off her coat, causing my jaw to drop.

"Rosemary-chicken breast, mashed potatoes, green beans, rolls, and you for dinner."

"Sounds good."

"Oh trust me it is."

I pulled out her chair for her so that she could have a seat at the table. Pushing her chair in, I took a seat next to her. She must have been hungry because she bowed her head and immediately began eating the food. I poured her a glass of wine and poured myself a shot of Hennessy.

"Damn, you eating like you haven't had anything to eat all day."

"Sorry, I was really hungry."

"No need to apologize, enjoy your food, there's more than enough."

I sat and admired her beauty as she ate. If we had met under different circumstances, I wouldn't mind having her as my wife. Looking at her, I wondered how could someone so pretty, get caught up in something so ugly. I even started to feel a little bad for her being I was the one that was going to have her sitting in jail, but she should have known the consequences that came behind swimming with sharks.

"You ready for dessert?" she asked as I downed my cup of Hennessy. She poured her another one and gulped it down as well.

She stood and unzipped her dress allowing it to fall to the floor. My dick started to rise watching her step out of her thong. Only in a pair of heels, she seductively walked towards my bedroom. In a trance, I watched her ass jiggle with every step she took. If I hadn't smacked and grabbed all on it, I would have thought that it was fake.

Walking to the cabinet, I grabbed a bottle of honey and whip cream. I could have sworn I saw some beams from a car shine through the window, but my dick was too hard and I wasn't thinking straight. When I walked in, the room Lala was laying in the bed with her legs wide open. I could see the cum oozing out of her pussy hole. Shaking the can of whip cream, I sprayed it all over her womanhood and bent down and had desert.

Chapter 17
Stacks

"Sir, we are unable to authorize you entrance onto the premises with out permission from Lala." I big, buff dude said as I tried to get inside my house.

"I know you don't know who the fuck I am and you're doing your job, but this is my fucking house! Somebody gonna let me in this bitch. Where is Lala?"

"She is not here?"

"Not here? Where the fuck she at?!" It was two in the fucking morning, wasn't shit open this late, but legs, so where the fuck could Lala possibly be and most importantly where the fuck was my kids! I was two seconds away from fucking dude up until Ralph noticed the commotion and came over.

"Big D, this Stacks homie he own this house so let him in," Ralph said.

"You sure?"

"Yes nigga let me the fuck in!" I yelled. He finally took heed to my warnings and opened up the entrance for me. I was surprised what Lala did to the house. She took the already big house I bought her and made it bigger.

"You good?" Ralph asked.

"Yeah, I'm straight good looking out."

"Fo sho. I'm out."

"Iight holla at ya'"

"No, doubt."

I walked through the pitch-black house and felt like a fucking stranger in my own home. Since Lala wasn't here to give me a tour, I decided to give myself one. I went through each room and was shocked that everything was pretty much the same, except the nursery was extended; one side was decorated in Mickey Mouse and the other side with Minnie Mouse. I sat in my kids' room and went through their things. Lala was definitely doing her thing with them because all of their things was on point and up to date. I definitely had me some mini bosses on my hand.

I picked up a picture of them and smiled. My babies were so damn cute. Amire looked just like me, and Amiracle was a spitting image of her mother. Picking up their baby book, I looked through the pages of events that I missed. I couldn't believe that I missed seven months of my kids' life, but now that I was home, I was going to make up for all that lost time.

My office pretty much looked the same except for the add on. I thought it was really cute how Lala added her things, instead of getting rid of mine. My man cave looked the same way I left it, bottle of Jack Daniels on the counter and all; it was as if in some weird way Lala knew I was going to return home.

I walked in our bedroom and everything again was pretty much the same. My clothes were still in my closet, which meant she ain't have no nigga in my house. Grabbing a pair of PJ bottoms, I laid it out on the bed with a pair of boxers and went to go take a nice, hot shower.

On a perfect day

I know that I can count on you

When that's not possible

Tell me can you weather the storm

'cause I need somebody who will stand by me

Through the good times and bad times

She will always, always be right there

Chorus:

Sunny days

Everybody loves them

Tell me

Can you stand the rain

Storms will come

This we know for sure

Can you stand the rain

I was singing a cappella to Boy II Men's *Can You Stand The Rain*, soaping up my body with the Irish Spring soap when I felt cold steel at the back of my head. Slowly turning around, Lala was standing there pointing a gun at me assuming that I was an intruder. She looked as if she had just been fucked and it caused my heart to drop.

Her hair was all over her head. Her dress wasn't fully zipped and through the sheer of the mesh I could see that she wasn't wearing any panties.

"What the fuck," she cried as she looked me in the eyes while still holding the gun.

"It's me baby, put the gun down."

"No, it can't be! I prepared your burial, I was there when they buried you!"

"Did you see my body?"

"No but y-"

"Then it wasn't me."

She then clicked the gun and pointed it at me again.

"So, if you wasn't dead where the fuck were you?" she asked with so much pain in her eyes.

"With Amanda," I answered. Her trigger finger started to shake and she was inches from pulling the trigger. "She kidnapped me."

"She kidnapped you?"

"Yes, while I was in a coma she staged the scene to make it look like the ambulance blew up, but she had me all along."

"That little bitch. I'mma kill her ass."

"I already handled that."

"Oh, my God, is it really you?"

"In the flesh baby."

I grabbed the gun from her hand, put the safety back on it and slid it across the bathroom floor. She jumped in my arms fully clothed with her arms wrapped around my neck. I could smell the nigga she was with all over her, so I put her down and undressed her. Throwing her dress on the ground, I made a mental note to burn it. Taking her sponge, I poured some of her body wash on it before lathering her body. I was not about to be hugged up on my bitch with her smelling like another nigga.

Once I noticed her tattoo of my name, I stopped and lifted her leg so that I could get a better look at it. When I was done washing her up, I grabbed the shampoo, poured some in my hand, and began washing her hair. The whole time she just stood there crying. I could see the guilt that was written all over her face. I didn't blame her for any of her actions, I was technically dead and she was free to do whatever she pleased.

"Where are my kids?" I asked breaking the silence

"In Orlando with Anna."

"Why are they in Orlando and who the fuck is Anna?"

"Anna is the nanny I hired to help me with them and they went on vacation."

"You needed help raising my kids?"

"Yes Stacks, raising twins alone and trying to work isn't easy."

"When are they coming home?"

"In a few days."

"Lala, let me ask you something," I said rinsing the shampoo out of her hair and grabbing the conditioner.

"What type of work do you do?"

"I own three clinics."

"How did you come up with the funds for your clinics."

"You left me enough money."

I was hoping that she was going to open up and tell me about her now running the cartel. If she wasn't ready to tell me then I wasn't going to beat it out of her. Although I had my job back, I was willing to still have her on my team as my partner. She was very good with flipping weight and making it worth more than it actually was.

I needed muscle like her on my team. After talking to Carla, I was able to get her to see things my way. I worked out a deal that her, her father, and my father was both happy with. No matter how tough or smart Lala thought she was, a war with the Lopez's was something we couldn't afford.

After making sure all traces of that nigga she was with were gone, I lifted her up against the wall and covered her mouth with mine.

"Mmmmmm," she moaned and I bit down gently and sucked on her tongue.

I made sure that the water from the shower was falling directly on us as I rammed my dick in her and began to fuck her.

"Oh gaaaaaaaaaaaaaaawd," she squealed with her eyes closed shut as I continued to hammer my dick in her pussy. I was putting a hurting on it in such a pleasurable way. I was going to fuck her until she tapped out, while teaching her a lesson for giving my pussy away.

"I'm about to nnnnnnnnnnut! Damn!" she called out squirting her warm juices all over me.

I was only in her for about a minute and she was creaming all over my dick. That only let me know that nigga she was fucking couldn't fuck her like I could. I flipped her over, raised one of her legs on the shower knobs, and entered her from the back using excessive force. I pinched her nipples and began twirling them between my fingers. Before I could ever reach over and play with her clit, she was nutting on my dick again.

Throwing her over my shoulders like a rag doll, I turned off the water and threw her on the bed. Drying her pussy with the towel, I knelt down in front of her and ate her out. It had been a while since I ate pussy and I was starving for that shit.

Spreading her lips, I started giving her nice, long licks, using the thickness of my tongue to apply pressure on her clit. It began to swell, so I wrapped my lips around it, and sucked it. She was on the verge of cumming again, but I flipped her over and began eating her from the back, sticking one of my fingers in her ass hole.

"Oh shit!" she cried as I bit down hard on her clit causing her to shiver "Please Stacks make me cum," she begged. I wasn't done with her yet. I still had plans on teasing her and making her beg me for mercy.

"Pleeeeeease!" She pleaded for me to bring her to that peak, but all I did was let it build up and stop. She was squirming in my mouth trying to get some friction applied to her clit, so that she could get her rocks off. I wasn't having that, she was on my time. I slowly licked and sucked on her pearl, stopping whenever I felt her near an orgasm.

"I swear if you don't make me nut now I'mma blow your fucking head off!" she snapped becoming tired of my games.

"You want to nut?"

"Yessss please."

I licked on her pussy faster, and sucked on it harder. Using my fingers, I shoved them in her wet slippery mound as my tongue played with her love button. I felt a gush of liquid fill my mouth and I sucked it all up, drinking every drop. She was breathing as if she just got done running a marathon, but I wasn't done with her yet, I still had to get mine off.

I locked each of her legs in the crook of my arms and pushed the back until they were touching the headboard. I positioned my dick in her hole and began deep stroking her. Loving the way her nut was coating my dick. I would go deep and pull it all the way out. Wrapping her legs around my waist, I bent down and whispered in her ears.

"Never give my pussy away, especially to a nigga that can't hit it the way daddy can."

With that said, I fucked her until she went crazy. I had to check her pulse a few just to make sure she was still breathing. She tapped out after her ninth nut, but I wasn't stopping until her nut count was in double digits. She was weak and I could feel her legs turn into noodles, but her pussy kept talking to me. I finally decided that she had enough. I stroked her nice and slow until we both climaxed.

"I love you, Lala," I said cuddling up with her.

"I love you, too," she faintly answered before she was out for the count. Daddy was home now!!

Chapter 18

Lala

When I came home from my date with Joey and heard sounds coming from my bathroom, I was ready to kill me a bitch. The closer I got to the bathroom, the more I thought I was going crazy. My heart was telling me that it was Stacks' voice in the Singing Boys II Men, but my mind told me it couldn't be because he was dead.

I had my gun to his head and ready to shoot the intruder's ass until I saw the tattoo on his back. My heart began beating fast and I felt my knees getting weak. When he turned around, I thought I had officially lost my mind and that it was time to check myself into the Henderson Psych Ward.

Hearing his voice, feeling his body next to mine, feeling his lips covering mine felt so surreal. I was finally in the arms of my man again and it felt so good. When he began to wash me off, I could tell that he realized that I was with another man. The way he looked at me with hurt in his eyes made me feel like shit. I had to remind myself that I did nothing wrong, that he was supposed to be dead, and it was okay for me to move on.

Watching him sleep, I didn't want to leave, but I had to. I knew with Stacks back now that he was going to be taking over, but until then, I still had my duties to fulfill. I tried to stand up, but my legs were so sore that it felt like I was going to fall on my face.

Last night Stacks definitely put a hurting on my kitty and left his mark. On my third attempt of getting out of bed, I was finally successful. I slowly moved around the room trying to get ready. I wanted to avoid waking him up and going through another line of questioning. I picked up a pen and left him a nice note, before heading down to my woman cave to shower up and get ready.

Dressed in a pair of pink and black graffiti jogging pants, a black crop top, my black Gucci heel boots, with my matching Gucci black leather jacket I was ready to hit the rode. Today was shipment day and I made it my business to be there on time. I wanted to see the product with my own eyes just to make sure I was getting my money's worth. I decided today I was going to ride my 2015 custom made princess hot pink and black Suzuki GSX 600 bike. Grabbing my helmet, I pulled my hair into a low ponytail then pulled it over my face. I started my bike and the guards opened the gates to let me out.

Bitches ain't shit, and they ain't sayin' nuthin'
A hundred muthafuckas can't tell me nuthin'
I beez in the trap, bee, beez in the trap
I beez in the trap, bee, beez in the trap

I jammed Nicki Minaj's *Beez In The Trap* as I zoomed in and out of traffic. I made it to the port in twenty minutes flat. Parking my bike, I punched in the code to the meat-packaging warehouse and waited. The shipment wasn't schedule to get here for another fifteen minutes, but I always liked to be at my location early, something I picked up from Stacks.

I looked outside and made sure that all of my security guards and sharp shooters were in place. Even though I was dealing with people that had been in the family for years, I still didn't trust them. I was a female, an easy target, so I had to always be a few steps ahead of the game.

Noticing that Ralph wasn't here yet, I hit the blue tooth speaker I had in my ear and gave him a call.

"Yoooo!"

"Where you at?"

"I'm on my way. I had to make a quick stop."

"Hurry up, drop is in ten minutes."

"I gotchu ma'. I'll be there in five."

Waiting for Ralph to come, I gave my stylist a call and informed him that I needed a new wardrobe for Stacks. I gave him the sizes and they type of clothing that Stacks liked. Stacks had more than enough clothes, but I needed to upgrade him.

After hanging up the phone with my stylist, I heard the code being punched in the door and Stacks walked in. At that very moment, I wished there was a hole that I could crawl into and hide, but there wasn't. I was going to kill Ralph for setting me up.

"The dropped was already taken care of," Stacks spoke as he wrapped his arms around my waist.

"How did you know?" I asked giving Ralph an evil glare.

"Papa told me."

"So, you spoke with him?"

"I saw him, I was in Columbia."

"Did you distribute?"

"Yup."

"Did you collect the money?"

"Yup."

"Did you swing by the traps?"

"Done."

I gave him a smile, and kissed him on the lips. A part of me was happy that he was home and I was now able to focus on my clinics and my kids, but the other half of me was going to miss being the head bitch in charge.

"I still want you on my team," Stacks said putting his hands in my back pockets.

"You do?"

"Yes, you my Bonnie right?"

"Always."

"We ride together."

"We die together," I said finishing our favorite line form Bad Boyz.

"Damn my bitch riding motorcycles and shit, that shit sexy as fuck."

"If you're a good boy I might let you fuck me on my bike," I flirted while whispering in his ear.

"Oh, yeah?"

"Yup!"

"Give me a ride then," he said putting his tongue in my mouth. I could taste the kush that he smoked as our tongues became acquainted.

"Get a room!" Ralph said waving his hands.

"Yo' I'm good, I'm riding with wifey."

"Iight, be easy."

"Peace."

Stacks continued to caress and kiss all over me until his dick was standing at attention.

"You gon' let me slide in real quick?"

"Here?"

"Yes, please, I'll make it worth it," he said and nibbled on my spot behind my ear.

Without waiting for my answer, he leaned me up against the metal door and pulled my pants down my ankles. Tooting my ass up towards him, I felt him slide in me and fuck me until I was squirting on his dick and he was spilling his seeds in me.

He pulled some napkins out of his pockets and we cleaned up before hopping on my bike and riding through the wind. His arms were wrapped securely around my waist as he sat behind me and whispered how sexy I looked whipping the bike around town.

Stopping at an IHOP, we had breakfast and enjoyed each other's company. I caught him up on everything that had been going on, leaving out Joey. I knew Stacks knew about the guy I was seeing; I just didn't feel like he was important enough to talk about.

Halfway through our conversation, my phone started to ring. My heart dropped seeing Joey's name flash across the screen. Putting on my poker face, I shrugged, ignored his call, and put my phone on silence. Stacks gave me a look as if he was going to ask me who was calling me, but he decided not to. I was glad he didn't ask, I wasn't prepared to go into details about the little fling I had with Joey.

Stacks suggested that we should go to Disney and meet up with the kids and Anna. Agreeing to his idea, I made our plans and informed Anna that we would be there in the morning. I was excited to have the kids meet Stacks for the first time. The moment that I thought would never occur was finally about to happen and all I could do was cry.

I thanked God over and over again for sending Stacks back and giving us a second chance. Now, my kids will be able to grow up knowing their father and I was willing to give up anything for that moment. I had to pinch myself a few times just to make sure that this moment was real.

After breakfast, we went home and packed for our trip, then we spent the remainder of the day in the house getting to know each other all over again. I wanted him all to myself before the kids came home and take up all of his attention.

I bet the neighbors know my name
Way you screamin scratchin yellin,
Bet the neighbors know my name
They be stressin while we sexin,
I bet the neighbors know my name
My name my name
I bet the neighbors know my name
My my my...

Stacks sung as in my ear as if he was Trey Songz himself. The way he was making me hoot and holler I was sure that my voice was going to be gone by the end of the night.

The next morning, we woke up and boarded the plan to Orlando. Anna and the kids were staying at the Nickelodeon Resort, so we had the driver drop us off there. When he got to their hotel room, I could hear the kids laugh and scream out as if they were having the time of their life. I looked over at Stacks and had to laugh at him because he looked a nervous wreck.

Using the key Anna left me at the front desk, I saw my babies crawling around. My heart sank because I wasn't there with them to witness this moment. Amire looked up and saw me and immediately crawled over to me. Amiracle crawled over to Stacks, stopped in front of him, and reached out her little arms so that he could pick her up.

He then reached for Amire and went to go sit on the couch with them. My heart melted as I watched the interaction with him, Amiracle was already team Stacks, but since Amire was such a mama's boy, it took him a few minutes before he finally warmed up to him.

"I thought their father died." Anna whispered in my ear.

"It's a long story."

"Well, chile, c'mon in the kitchen and explain it to me while I make breakfast. Let them babies bond with their daddy."

I watched Stacks play with them some more before going in the kitchen with Anna and explaining to her all the crazy events that took place. As Anna plated the last of the food, the story was complete and she was standing there looking at me with her mouth wide open.

"So, does this mean you won't be needing my services anymore?" she sadly asked.

"Of course, I'm going to be working at the clinic more now and Stacks is going back to his old job soon, so we will be needing you. Plus, the kids love you, I would never take them away from you."

"Good, for a moment there I was scared."

"No need to be, Ms. Anna, you're family now and we love you."

"I love you guys, too. Now, go call your husband and let him now breakfast is ready."

When I made it back in the living room of the suite, Stacks was knocked out with both of the babies sprawled across his chest. Taking out my camera, I snapped a picture of them. That picture was so cute that I was going to print it and have it framed.

Anna came out to see what was taking us so long and when she saw them laying across the couch, she grabbed a blanket and draped it over them.

"Let him bond with his babies. I guess it's just you and I for breakfast."

"I guess so," I replied and walked back into the kitchen. I said grace, then grabbed my plate and began to eat.

I made a mental note to find a church home for my family. It was only right that as a family we invited

Christ into our lives, without him none of this would have been possible. My phone began vibrating, it was Joey again. I haven't figured out what I was going to say to him, but I knew that I had to get rid of him before Stacks did.

Chapter 19

Lisa

I was happy that Stacks was finally back. My Lala deserved to have her man back with her. Like Ralph I wasn't too fond of the Idris Elba lookalike she was fucking with and I was happy he was about to become a distant memory. Now that Lala had her man back, I was determined to get mine back.

No matter how much I tried to stay away from Ralph and move on, he wouldn't allow me to. He would pop up at my house unannounced and even on some of my dates. Half of the dudes in Miami didn't want to fuck with me because of him. So tonight was the night, I was going to pop up at his house and if that bitch Kandi or any other bitch for that matter was there, I was putting their ass out.

Oiling up my legs, I slipped my mini skirt over my bare ass, and pulled the half shirt over my head. Spraying my special spots with my Viva La Juicy perfume, I placed two Altoids on my tongue and headed out to my car.

The drive to Ralph's house had me very anxious. I kept contemplating whether I should call him to let him know I was on my way or not. The blue, white, and red lights flashing behind me brought my focus on the rode. I was so consumed in my thoughts that I didn't realize that I ran a stop sign.

Slowing down my car, I pulled over. I quickly applied more of my MAC gloss to my lips, hoping it was a male officer that was pulling me over. There was a tap at my window, so I hit the button allowing it to roll down.

"Ma'am, did you notice you ran the stop sign?"

"Yes sir, and I am sorry. My boyfriend just broke up with me and I have so much on my mind," I sadly replied.

"May I please have you license and registration?" he asked with sympathy in his eyes for me.

I unbuckled my seatbelt and reached over to my glove compartment, raising my leg a little bit so that my skirt could rise and show off glimpse of my ass. I heard him inhale, and then clear his throat. So to fuck with him even more, I leaned over further, showing off more of my ass. I was acting as if I was really looking for the envelope that held my documents.

When I was sure that his dick was hard in his pants, I sat up straight and handed him the folder along with my license. He walked back to his car with my information and had me waited for a good fifteen minutes. That was a little off to me and my gut was telling me something wasn't right.

Twenty minutes later, he returned with my documents and handed them to me.

"Have a nice night and try watching for those stop signs," he said winking and then walking away.

I search for a ticket, but couldn't find one. If he wasn't back there writing me a ticket then what the fuck took him so long with my shit. I asked myself feeling as if something was really fishy. As I was about to put the envelope back, I saw that he wrote his number on the back of it. Taking my registration out, I ripped up the envelope and threw it out the window. I didn't fuck with the alphabet boys like that.

Pulling up in front of Ralph's house, there wasn't any sign of him being there. I parked my car and walked to the door. I knocked a few times and came to the conclusion that no one was home. I was pissed at myself for returning his key.

"You trying to break inside my house," Ralph voice boomed from behind me

"I came by to say hello."

"Never heard of calling before you show up to some one's house."

"Do you ever call before you come over?"

"Nah. But I gotta check up on you because every time I turn around, you fucking with a lame ass nigga."

"I used to fuck with you, so what does that makes you?"

"The realest nigga you ever had."

"Shut up!"

"So, to what do I owe this visit?"

"Nothing just was in the neighborhood and wanted to say hi."

"In that little ass skirt?"

"Yup!" I smirked.

"What's under that skirt?" he asked pinning me up against his front door.

"Why don't you check and see."

He put his hand under my skirt and groaned when he felt my bare ass. Rubbing my perfectly round ass in his hand, he licked my earlobe.

"You tryna make me body a nigga?" he asked as he slipped his hand in my pussy.

"Why you trying to kill someone over something that doesn't belong to you?"

"You will always be mine."

"So, we ain't together?"

"We're working on it."

"Daaaaaamn!" I moaned as I came all over his fingers.

Hiking my skirt above my waist, I wrapped my legs around his waist and allowed him to enter me.

"Damn you so wet," he whispered in my ears as he dug deep inside me instantly hitting my G-spot. "Why you so wet?" he asked and yanked my hair back, exposing my neck. He planted soft kisses all over before sucking real hard. The stingy sensation only brought more pleasure to me and I was near my peak.

"Damn like that?" he asked as I squeezed my pussy tight around his dick.

High beans from a light pulling into his driveway shined on us, but we were too engrossed in pleasure on another to pay it any mind. I held onto him tight as he began to stroke me with so much force. He was on the verge of coming, and I wanted to come along with him. Spreading my legs wider, I rotated my hips as we fucked each other as if we were in our own world not paying the person that stood there watching us no mind.

"I'm gone for a few weeks and this what you do?" Kandi asked, as Ralph emptied his seeds in me and I came shortly afterwards.

"What are you doing here?" Ralph asked zipping up his pants and adjusting my skirt.

"I had to talk to you, but you wasn't answering the phone."

"Kandi, I told you what it was. Man."

"I know, but I'm pregnant," she replied shocking the hell out of me.

I looked up Ralph in the eyes pleading for him to deny it being his child. I waited for him to tell her to get the fuck out of his face, but he never did, which only confirmed that there was a possibility that the child she was carrying was his. Tears began to burn my eyes, blurring my vision. I quickly tried to blink them away, not wanting to show Kandi any weakness, but it was pointless. I was hurt; there was no way to hide it.

"Go inside," Ralph said unlocking his door for me. My legs wouldn't allow me to walk, so he carried me inside, placed me on the couch, and went outside closing the door behind him.

Unable to hold in my tears anymore, I laid on the couch and cried my heart out not giving a fuck who heard me. I was really hurt. Love seemed to always have a problem with me finding it, because once I did, it seemed to always find a way to bite me in the ass.

I could hear them arguing. Ralph was demanding that he got a DNA test before he took on any responsibility of being a father to any child. She shouted back that he wasn't singing that tune when he was all in her pussy hitting it raw. They continued to bicker back and forth, until I heard her car door slam close, the roaring of her ignition, and then the sound of the car burning rubber.

Ralph stayed outside for a few minutes gathering his thoughts before finally coming inside. I heard him close and lock the door, then the alarm beep. The sound of his footsteps were getting closer and closer until they finally stopped. I felt him standing over me as I laid on the couch curled up in a fetal position.

"Baby, I'm so sorry," he said lifting me up, and then sitting back on the couch with me on his chest.

"Sorry for what?" I whispered.

"For fucking up."

"Where does that leave us?"

"I'm still here, I'm not going anywhere."

"It hurts," I cried.

"I know and I'm so sorry for causing you any pain."

I just laid there in his arms and cried until exhaustion took over me and I fell asleep in his arms.

Chapter 20
Ralph

Waking up to an empty bed really had me feeling some type of way. A nigga was in love for the first time in a long time and I wasn't even able to be with her because of fucked up situations. I knew if Kandi's baby turned out to be mines it was a wrap for Lisa and I. I wasn't they type of nigga that would let their kids suffer, so if it was mine I was going to be there for him or her.

I raw dogged Kandi one time. It was one night that I was gone off some high grade, drunk, and I popped an X pill. That night I was fucking Kandi imagining she was Lisa and the thought of a condom slipped my mind.

"The number you have reached had recently been disconnected."

The lady on the other end of the phone repeated in my ear as I tried to call Lisa. I couldn't believe that she actually changed her number. I was on my way to go handle her, but I forgot today was the day I was going to show Stacks his gift that I had waiting for him. He had no idea that I had Bear tied up begging to be put out of his misery. I made sure he was tortured everyday, but not enough for him to die.

"Wake up nigga, today your lucky day," I said slapping him behind the head.

"I swear you better kill me," Bear words slurred through his busted lips. His whole front row of teeth were missing.

"I'm not gonna kill you, Stacks is," I laughed.

"Well, tell that fuck nigga to hurry up!" he spat.

I was about to deck his ass until I heard the roar of motorcycles coming into the building. Out of nowhere two bikes appeared in front of where Bear and I was standing then stopped. *Stacks and Lala on some Bonnie and Clyde type shit*; I thought as I watched them take off their helmets.

"My nigga, my nigga," I said giving Stacks dap.

"Is this that nigga Bear?" he asked getting excited.

"Yeah, he's all yours."

"Bear, where you been nigga?" Stacks asked standing in front of him.

"Nigga quit the small talk, just make sure ain't no pulse when you done cause' when I come back nigga I'm coming back with full force."

"Look at this Kevin Hart ass nigga over here telling jokes and shit. Ain't no way your ass coming back when I'm done with you."

"Shoot then pussy!"

WHAM!

Lala punched him in the face causing blood to splatter everywhere.

"Respect my nigga, pussy!"

"Fuck you bitch!"

"For a dead nigga, you got a lot of balls," she replied and pulled out two pistols, handing one to Stacks.

I stood off to the side and lit my blunt, taking a long pull; I held it in then blew it out. I continued to blow the dro while I watched what was going to happen.

"Any last words before I send your ass to hell."

"Nah, but I'll make sure to eat Donna's pussy real good when I arrive," he laughed, spitting his blood on Stack's shoe.

I watch Lala give him a head nod. Simultaneously, I watched as both of them unloaded their guns in Bear's body. The force of the bullets were so strong that it knocked him out of the chair. I watched as they reloaded their guns and stood directly in front of him then unloaded their full clip in his head. His head split open like a watermelon as all of his brain matter spilled on to the ground. That shit was the most gruesome murder I had ever seen.

"Pick that fuck nigga up, burn him, and then pour his grimey ass down the sewer," Lala demanded.

"Got damn my bitch bad!" Stacks said smacking her on the ass. "You heard my first lady, handle that shit!!"

WHAM!!

"That's for Lisa. I love you, but you need to get it together!" Lala said hitting my ass with a mean one. I could taste the blood filling up in my mouth; I spit it out and sucked on my lips trying to add pressure to stop the bleeding. I ain't gon' lie I really did deserve that shit. She handed me a key to Lisa's house and I accepted it. I watched them in awe as they got on their bikes and left the building.

"Y'all hear the boss, clean this shit up!"

I monitored them as they followed Lala's orders. Once he was burned to ashes and his ashes were poured down the sewer, I left and went to Lisa's house. When I got there, I knew she was home because the lights were on in her house and her car was parked out front.

I surveyed the house to make sure she wasn't with nobody; the way I was feeling I was liable to body a nigga. Puffing on a blunt, I sat back and rehearsed what I was going to say.

Using the key Lala gave me, I let myself inside her house. I was immediately smacked with a huge cloud of smoke. She must have really been stressing because she was smoking on some Loud. Following the smoke clouds and loud music, it led me to the bathroom.

Pushing the door all the way open, my heart broke. Lisa was lying in a full tub, puffing a blunt while her tears added more water to the tub. She was singing along with Monica asking if she should stay or go.

Leaning my tall frame up against the door, I took in the scene before I realized that I damaged this girl's heart. It wasn't intentionally, I didn't mean to, but I did. I felt like shit for being the reason she was soaking in a tub filled with tears, and I was going to make it my business to make things right between us.

"How the fuck did you get in my house," Lisa said as she looked at me with her bloodshot eyes.

"I used my key."

"Well, use that shit to lock the door on your way out." She got out the tub, wrapped her body in a towel, and walked past me. Following her to her bedroom, I grabbed her by her wrist and pulled her into my arms.

"Let me go!" she yelled.

"No."

"I hate you!"

"I know."

"Why does bad shit always have to happen to me?"

I held her tight as she vented and cried in my arms. She cried until she couldn't cry anymore.

"Let me make this right."

"You can't," she said just above a whisper.

"Watch me," I said laying her body down on the bed.

I removed the towel that was covering her body and spread her legs wide. My tongue zeroed in on her clit as I used the tip of it to tease it. I could feel her wetness ooze down my chin as her legs began to shake. I flipped her so that she was sitting directly on my face.

Locking my fingers around her waist, I held a long conversation with her pussy. I made my tongue real stiff and rotated her hips into my mouth. When I felt that first contraction around my tongue, I used my fingers to squeeze on her pearl. Her body began to violently shake as her love came down and damn near drowned me. Opening my mouth wide, I placed it in her hole and sucked the rest of her sweet nectar.

She looked up at me with tears in her eyes as I entered her soul. With each stoke I made; I apologized and asked for her forgiveness. I held on to her tight as I slowly made love to her. The only sounds that could be heard were the sounds of me dipping in and out of her wetness.

I continued to poke at her G-spot as she mumbled under her breath. The more I hit her spot the gushier her pussy became and the harder it made my dick. Her pussy lips swallowed my dick and I swear I started having an outer body experience.

"Fuck!" I growled as I felt my nut build up. Not wanting to go out like a bitch, I bit down hard on my lip to prevent me from nutting. I could taste the blood in my mouth, so I focused on trying to stop the bleeding just to get my mind off of how good the pussy was.

When a gush of liquid drenched my dick, I released myself in her and collapsed. After catching my breath, I went in the bathroom and washed my dick off. Grabbing a rag, I wet it in warm water and went to wash Lisa off.

"You hungry?" I asked. She nodded her head up and down.

I went to the kitchen and looked through the pile of menus and decided to order us some Chinese food. After putting in our order, my phone started to ring. I made a mental note to go see Kandi before I turned off my personal phone.

I took a seat outside and puffed on a blunt while I waited for the delivery guy. I had so much on my mind that I felt myself going crazy. The more I puffed the calmer I became and the better I was able to sort things out. I felt bad for the way I spoke to Kandi and I was going to make it my business to make up with her. If it was in fact my baby she was carrying, I wanted us to at least be on good terms. I already had a troubled baby mama and I wasn't trying to have a second one.

"Delivery," the Chinese man said as he brought me back to reality. "$32.50." He handed me the brown paper bags. I went in my pockets, pulled of a fifty-dollar bill, and told him to keep the change.

I went inside and placed the food on the counter. Grabbing two plates, I made us each a plate of food. When I entered the room with the food, Lisa was just getting out of the shower. The robe that she had on was real short, leaving little to the imagination. My dick got rock hard when she bent over to apply lotion to her legs showing off her ass cheeks. Walking up behind her, I smacked her hard on the ass before placing the food on the nightstand.

"Did you get me an extra side of orange chicken?" she asked sitting on the chess she had at the foot of her bed

"I gotchu ma."

"Why you still here?"

"Damn a nigga done gave you that good dick and now you trying to put me out?"

"Ralph, that's three baby mamas!"

"What difference does it makes? I'm still going to handle mine as a father and be able to fulfill my duties as your man."

"That's not the point."

"Then what's the point?" I asked.

"What if I want to have a baby, too, then what that makes me baby mama four?"

"No, that will make you my wife. I have plans of marrying you and that's real," I honestly replied.

She just looked at me with a blank expression on her face and went to eating her food. When I was done eating, I took my plate to the kitchen. I entered the bathroom so that I could take a nice hot shower to cool my mind down a bit. While in the shower, I felt a cool draft hit my body, then a pair of hands grab my dick. I closed my eyes and allowed my future wife to suck my stress away.

Chapter 21

Ashley

Karma is a real bitch, I thought as I sat at the island puffing on my blunt. It was still hard for me to believe that Lala was fucking my man. I guess it was my payback for all the times I fucked her man. I was livid as fuck! Here I was wearing this nigga's engagement ring, carrying his fucking baby, and he chose to fuck Lala.

The thought of him doing the things to her that he did to me caused me to become sick to my stomach. Unable to control the contents of my stomach, I rushed to the bathroom and threw up everything. The shoe wasn't really fitting good now that it was on the other foot.

I knew I should have killed Lala. I should have fucked her whole life up when I had to chance to, but I decided that her having to raise kids without their father would be punishment enough, but boy was I wrong.

Brushing my teeth, I made a promise to myself that I was going to handle the bitch. As far as Joey, I was just going to give his ass the benefit of the doubt and let him get a pass this time. I still wanted to know how the hell them two linked up.

Going in his office, I tried to open the file cabinet where he kept all of his important case documents. Before Stacks died, my main purpose of us teaming up was for him to bring down Stacks and for me to kill Lala, but since the death of Stacks, he stopped working on the case.

Curiosity began to get the best of me when I was able to go through all the cabinets except one that was locked. I tried to use a paper clip to jimmy it open, but it wouldn't budge.

Retrieving my phone from my back pocket, I made a phone call to my cousin and asked him to meet me at the Steak N' Shake. I also made a phone call to my aunt and asked her if she was able to keep my son for me for the weekend. I was feeling like them niggas on Scooby Doo, determined to get to the bottom of this mystery.

As I was getting up to leave his office, I heard the fax machine beep and papers begin to come through.

Looking through the papers, I didn't see anything really important except case files. I started to put everything back, until I saw a cover page to a fax that read,

Detective Armstrong,
Enclosed are the information that you requested on Lisa.

At first, I thought it was another Lisa until I saw the picture of the bitch. Gathering all the papers that had the information on Lisa, I folded them and put them in my backpack. I made sure that all of the other papers were in the same order it came in and neatly stacked before leaving his office.

Taking the papers out of my back pocket, I entered my room and sat on my bed. Unfolding them, I began to read the information that was obtained by the squad's P.I. I had to put the papers down and pick them back up just to make sure I was reading everything correctly.

Re-reading those lines again, my mouth formed in an "O" as shocked filled my body. I just sat there looking at the paper as if it was infected with some type of disease. I couldn't believe this shit!!

Chapter 22

Kandi

My last tear just fell from my eyes

Told myself that I wasn't going to cry no more

(you did what you did, it is what it is) and that's why I

walked out the door.

Moved on with my life, but not really

Spent too much time wondering how could you

(you do this to us while we we're in love) I guess I

was thinking too much

I was thinking that the sex had your love

You never could get enough cause I kept it hot

I listen to you tell me your dreams

And your fears

I wiped your tears

I was there and this is why this is hurting me

Why her? Why her?

Did I get on your nerves?

Did I give you too much that you couldn't handle my love?

Why her? Why her?

I lay across the hotel's bed and allowed the words of Monica's *Why Her* to take over me as my tears flooded the pillow. I was supposed to be happy that I was pregnant with my first child by the man that I loved, but instead I was all in my feelings. I really thought that Ralph and I had something, but he was right we never actually made it official.

I was living in his house when I came down from school, he was paying for my tuition, buying me things, showing me off to his friends, but that didn't qualify me as he girl. I guess if I swung around a pole instead of going to school to follow my dreams, I would have been a candidate.

I was nothing like my surroundings. Ever since I was a little girl, I knew what I wanted and I was going to go for it. I was going to be a fashion designer and my clothing was going to be worn on fashion models and at fashion shows. I had dreams on creating looks for celebrities. I started working at the trap for Ralph just to make that dream a reality.

I didn't come from money, so I wasn't able to afford to attend a top high fashion school in New York. When one of the corner boys suggested I worked at the trap my first answer was hell no, but when I saw the amount of money that I could be making I was all in.

While working for Ralph, I did have a little crush on him. He was so smooth, sexy, and attentive. He always looked out for everyone with hefty bonuses and he never tried to sex up any of the girls that worked for him, although if he tried, we all would have let him.

The day he saved me from working in that hell hole was the day I fell in love with him. When I went off to school, he would call me to check on my grades and to make sure that I had everything I needed. I was what he called his little investment. He was investing in my career so that I wouldn't become a product of my environment. The days I would come down, he would allow me to stay over and kick it with him, by that time he had just broken up with his girlfriend Lisa.

I got so comfortable around him that I forgot to ask him where I stood and now to know that I am pregnant with his child and we had no future together hurt me to the core.

A soft knock on the door interrupted me from my thoughts. Getting up from the bed, I answered the door and faced the guy that hurt me so bad. I stepped to the side and allowed him to come inside before closing the door. He took a seat on the sofa, took his hat off, and rubbed it across his freshly cut Lil Boosie fade.

I sat back and watched him in awe. He was dressed in a white shirt, with baby blue, and grey writing that read, *It Cost to be the Boss*. He matched it up with a pair of light blue True Religion jeans, with a brand new pair of Jordan Retro 11 Legend Blues.

The scent of his cologne was causing my body to do things that caused me to be in my current predicament.

"I'm sorry," he spoke above a whisper.

I turned off the radio, so that I was able to hear him clearly.

"I didn't mean for things to end up like this. It's my fault though. I should have kept it all the way one hundred with you." He spoke with his head still down. "I love Lisa and I want to make it work between us. However if in fact that is my baby you are carrying, I want to be in his or her life, too."

"Why do you keep saying if?!" I snapped. "This is your child!"

"That's what your lips say."

"And it's the fucking truth! You act like I'm some hood rat that you picked up off the street. I was working for you trying to get my shit together to better my life! I wasn't out here tricking for a dollar, or trying to bag the highest paid dope boy! If that were the case, I wouldn't have been putting my freedom on the line bagging a few bricks! Not once since we been *kicking it* have I stopped going to school. I never let the money, cars, clothes, or jewelry get to my fucking head! The fact that you practically run Miami didn't faze me because all that shit don't matter! So, don't sit up here and try to talk to me like I'm some two-dollar hoe. This is your fucking baby!!" I yelled and started sobbing uncontrollably.

"Come here," he said extending his hand out to me. I walked in his embrace and he held me while I cried.

"I'mma do right by you and my seed ma believe that."

"What about us?"

"That's complicated," he said.

"Why does it have to be? We can raise our child together as a family. We can give our baby something we never had."

"I'm trying to work it out with Lisa."

"But Lisa can't love you like I can," I responded before kissing his neck.

"Chill," he moaned as I began licking and sucking on his earlobes.

Not paying his weak attempts to stop me any mind, I pushed him on the bed and mounted him. Lifting his shirt, I licked him from his nipples down to his belly button. I used my teeth to unbuckle his belt and unzipped his pants.

Slipping my tongue in the slit of his boxers, I played with the head of his penis before stuffing it all in my mouth. I was sucking his dick like I had something to prove. I was determined to become the first lady in his life and if I had to suck and fuck all the thoughts of Lisa out of his mind, I was going to do it.

"OH, SHIT!" he growled as I slurped on his dick making it as messy as possible. I allowed my saliva to coat his dick before I hungrily sucked it all back up. I could feel the veins in his dick bulge as he was nearing his orgasm. I used all of my jaw muscles and sucked him up until he spilled my unborn child's brothers and sisters down my throat.

Swallowing them, I reached under my dress in one quick motion and snatched off my thong. My pussy was like a Lil Cesar's Pizza, Hot N' Ready as I slid down his pole and fucked him until he was team Kandi. Lisa who?

Chapter 23
Lala

"Bitch we about to turn the fuck up tonight," I said as I prepped the fruit for the hunch punch.

"Yessss bitch it's about to be a movie!!" Lisa replied while rolling the blunts. I was glad that she was now feeling better because I was about five seconds away from putting a bullet in Ralph's ass brother or not.

Putting the watermelons, orange, pineapples, limes, and strawberries in a bowl, I added some fruit juice and some Vodka to it. I put some ice in the cups and poured us both a drink. Before I could sip on my drink, I was hit with a wave of nausea. Running to the bathroom, I threw up everything I consumed for the day.

"Ump!" Lisa said one she walked inside the bathroom.

"Ump what?" I asked rinsing my mouth out.

"Bitches pregnant and shit but that ain't none of my business," she said before sipping her drink.

"I'm not pregnant."

"Let EPT tell it," she said and handed me a pregnancy test.

"I'm not about to take this test because I am not pregnant, so lets hurry up and get ready so we can go," I snapped while undressing so that I could get in the shower.

"Damn yo ass hormonal already."

"Shut up and get out," I yelled over the running water.

As soon as I heard the door shut, I burst into tears. It was not that I didn't like the thought of carrying Stacks' baby. It was that I wasn't sure who the father was. The night I slept with Joey, we had a slip up and then I came home and slept with Stacks, so there was a fifty, fifty chance that the baby I was carrying wasn't Stacks.

I knew this would ruin our family, so to avoid confusion; I planned on getting rid of the baby all together if I was in fact pregnant.

After my shower, I wasn't really in the partying mood anymore; I just went along with everything because I didn't want to let Lisa down. Today was supposed to be a girl's night out and I didn't want to spoil the night plus I didn't want her to think that I thought her accusations was true. Putting on my game face, I existed the bathroom and went inside the guestroom. Lisa was sitting on the bed waiting while smoking on a blunt as she waited for me. I grabbed the blunt from her and smoked it.

"I'm not keeping it if I am."

"Is it for Joey?"

"Possibly."

We sat there in silence passing a blunt back and forth. We were both in our feelings as we allowed our thoughts to take over us. Three blunts later, we got ready and headed out to the club. Tonight we were throwing it up at LIV; it was supposed to be a movie so it was a must that the two baddest bitches in Miami showed face.

The moment we hit the scene, the line for the club was wrapped around two blocks. It was so bad that Miami Dade Police Department was there taking people out of the line due to it being a fire hazard. There was no way in hell I was going to stand in line wearing these six thousand dollars Giuseppe Zanotti pumps. Lisa and I walked to the door and the red velvet rope opened up for us.

Taking a seat in our VIP section, we ordered our drinks and began to peep out the scene. Everybody that showed up came to dress to kill. Even the section 8 females were even killing the game in the outfits they bought from selling their babies' food stamps.

I was taking shots back to back when the DJ started spinning Bobby Shmurda's new hit *Bobby Bitch*. The whole club went dumb. Not wanting to mix in with the crowd wearing all this ice on me, I decided to shake my ass in our VIP section. I was in love with Bobby ol sexy ass, so whenever I heard his music I got silly with it.

The DJ decided to slow it down and started playing Ciara's *Body Party*. Holding onto the rail, I started grinding my hips. I was so high and a little tipsy that when I felt a pair of arms around my waist, I started grinding faster. I felt his dick starting to rise, so I bent over and started moving my hips like a snake.

"So, you just use me to catch your nut then disappear?" Joey whispered in my ears.

"It wasn't even like that," I said softly my words slurring.

"Then how was it?" he asked as I continued swaying my body to the beat of the music.

"I have a man."

"A man?"

"Yes nigga you heard her. She have a man, so get the fuck off her for I put three in ya' dome," Stacks calmly said and leaned against the rail.

I instantly began to sober up hearing his voice. My heart started to beat fast and I could feel my palms begin to sweat. I felt the grip that Joey had around my waist loosen as he looked in Stacks' eyes with shock written all over his face. It was as if he'd seen a ghost.

I pleaded with my eyes for Joey not to say anything that was going to send Stacks over the edge and have his body in a casket. Joey gave us one last look before walking away. I silently thanked the Lord as I exhaled the breath that I was holding in.

"You know dude?" Stacks asked me while looking me in the eyes.

"Yes," I answered. I wanted so badly to lie, but I learned from past experiences that lying to Stacks wasn't the smartest thing to do.

"Where you know him from?"

"We went on a few dates."

"Was that all? Just a few dates?"

"Yeah, nothing serious," I nervously answered.

"Did you have sex with him?"

"Does it matter? You we're supposedly dead!"

"It don't matter, but I still would like to know."

"Yes."

"How many times?"

"Two," I answered praying that he was done asking me questions. He simply just nodded his head and walked away. I was no longer feeling the vibe, so Lisa and I left for the night. Anna was staying over our house because of the renovations being done to her house, so I decided to cool it over at Lisa's house for the night.

By the time we reached Lisa's house, my phone was dead, so I put it in the charger and went to use the bathroom. I looked over at the EPT test that Lisa left on the counter and decided to just get it over with.

Squatting over the stick, I peed on it and sat it under the sink. I didn't want to risk Lisa barging in the bathroom and yelling at my results like she did the first time. Discarding the box, I went to the room and powered on my phone. My phone instantly began to light up with notifications as if it was the Fourth of July.

Scrolling through my messages, I had ten from Joey demanding that I give him an explanation, but none from Stacks. I thought that was very odd, so I called him to only get his voicemail. After attempting to call him with no avail, I threw my phone down on the bed. My phone then began ringing; I knew it wasn't Stacks because his assigned ring tone didn't play. Looking at the caller ID, I contemplated if I wanted to answer the phone or not. Taking a deep breath, I decided to face the music.

"Hello?"

"I really feel played."

"Joey, let me explain."

"I'm listening."

Just as I was about to give him an explanation, the timer on my phone began buzzing; signaling that the results of the pregnancy test was in.

"Hold on one moment," I said walking towards the bathroom to retrieve the test. I slowly counted to five before flipping it over and reading the results.

"Lala?!" I heard Joey call out to me from the other end of the phone, but all I could do was look at the test with tears in my eyes. He continued to yell out my name until I heard a female call out his name and then the line went dead.

I walked inside Lisa's room and cuddled with her under the sheets. My body shook as I cried. I rubbed my belly and apologized to my unborn child for what I was about to do.

"You're pregnant?" Lisa asked as she held me. I nodded my head and continued to cry.

Chapter 24

Joey

I was shocked to see that Stacks was actually alive and not dead. How was that possible? I didn't know. If someone would have told me that he was alive, I would of looked at them the same way my father was looking at me now. But seeing him with my own two eyes was something totally different.

"So you're trying to tell me that Stacks is alive?" my father asked me for the tenth time.

"Yes he is alive and well I seen him with my own two eyes," I assured him.

"This is un-fucking-believable. Before I bring anything to the mayor, I need more proof," he said before taking a sip of his black coffee. "How far are you on getting the information on Lisa?" Here we are in the middle of breaking the biggest case that the city of Miami has ever seen and he was worrying about Lisa.

"I have the P.I working on it for me."

"Good. When you get the information, I want you to present it to me immediately."

"Yes sir."

I was overwhelmed with the work that had to be done, but I was determined to bring Stacks down this time. I sent a text to the officer that I had tailing Lala to get her location so that I could take over watching her. He texted me the address to a woman's clinic that was three blocks away form the station.

When I arrived to the clinic, Lala was getting in her car and pulling off. I waited until she was completely out of sight and went inside to see why she was visiting an abortion clinic.

"Hello, I'm Detective Armstrong and someone that I am investigating was a patient here and I was just wondering why," I said to the front desk nurse and showed her my badge.

"Do you have a warrant?" she asked.

"No but…"

"Detective Armstrong, all of our information on our patients are confidential, unless you have a court order then there is nothing that I can tell you."

"Not even if it came with a price?"

"Are you trying to bribe me detective?"

"No, I'm going to reward you for helping me out."

She thought about it for a little bit before hitting the space bar on her computer.

"What is the name of the patient?"

"Lala Williams."

I watched as she typed on the keyboard.

"She has an appointment with us for next week."

"To do what?"

"Look around detective, you're smart enough to figure that part out."

"Thanks," I said peeling three hundred dollar bills out of my wallet and handing them to her. She looked around before discreetly placing the money in her bra and went back to typing away on the keyboard.

Sitting in my car, I was able to put two and two together. Lala was pregnant with my child and she was trying to end the pregnancy because of Stacks. By the way she was looking at the club, I was able to conclude that he knew nothing about me, which led me to believe that he knew nothing about her pregnancy.

I thought back to the last time we had sex and how we didn't use any protection. The thought of Lala having my child sucked out of her with a vacuum made my stomach turn. Although Ashley was pregnant with my child, I still felt uneasy having another one of my flesh and blood murdered.

I picked up my phone and called Lala, and like she had been doing for the past few days, I was sent to voicemail again. I was going to make her talk to me one way or another. It was my child too and I felt that I should have a say so on whether it lived or died.

ME: *I know you're pregnant with my child. I also know that you made an appointment at the Women's Clinic. I'm assuming that the baby is not for this man that you all of a sudden have and that you're trying to get rid of it before he finds out. Whatever the case maybe you need to find a way to contact me before I come for you.*

I sent Lala a text letting her know that I was no longer playing these games with her anymore. My phone beeped and I smiled knowing that I was going to get her attention with that text.

Tapping on the message icon, it was a multimedia message with the information that I requested on Lisa. I clicked on the link so that I was able to download the file. While the file was downloading, I got a text from Ashley informing me that she was stuck at our son's daycare with a flat tire. I placed the phone in the passenger's seat and headed towards my son's school.

It took me about fifteen minutes to make it to the daycare. When I finally did, I spotted Ashley leaning up against her car.

"Why didn't you call Triple A?"

"I did, but they wouldn't assist me because I didn't have my card with me."

"Didn't I always tell you to leave your card in your wallet?"

"Joey, now is not the time to argue. It is hot as hell out here and I just want to go home and lay down. I'm going to go sit in your car," she said and walked off before I could say anything.

I changed her tire in record timing. I noticed that her oil lights were on, so I went in the trunk and got the two bottles of oil that I left in there in case of an emergency. Filling up her car with oil, I went to put the half bottle of oil back in her trunk when I saw Jimmy's card next to one of her Gucci pumps. I was confused as to why my brother's card was in her trunk. Putting it in my pocket, I closed the trunk and went to my car to go and get her.

"You're all set," I said taking a seat in the driver's side.

"Thank you, are you heading home?"

"I will in a little bit."

"Ok, well see you later," she said as she leaned over to give me a kiss.

I watched her get in her car and pulled off. Picking up the phone, I checked to see if Lala ever responded to any of my texts. She hadn't, so I went to read the file I was sent, but for some reason the file was deleted. I tried to go back to the link to download it again, but it wouldn't allow me to. Sending the P.I. a text, I told him to resend me the link. Resting my head against the headrest, my mind went back to the card that I found in Ashley's truck. I dialed the number that was printed on the back of it.

You've reached Jimmy at J&R Private Investigations, sorry I missed your call, but if you leave a brief message with your name and number I'll be sure to give you a call back.

I know I hadn't spoken to my brother in a while, but the last time I spoke with him he was in the army not running a private investigation firm. I left him a voicemail saying that I would like to meet up with him. It was finally time that we sat and talked. I could probably use his help with the whole Lala and Stacks situation.

Chapter 25
Stacks

"Fuck me daddy!" Lala screamed as I pinned her legs back with my arms and started giving her deep strokes. I felt myself melting in her pussy with every thrust I made.

"Oh, damn!" I groaned feeling her pussy get wetter and wetter. Lala was known for having good pussy, but this what she had between her legs at the moment wasn't just good pussy. It was that shoot a nigga in the head for looking at your bitch wrong type of pussy. The deeper I went, the wetter she got and the hotter her pussy became. *Lala's pregnant,* I thought as I emptied my seeds in her.

"Damn, that was some good dick," she said as she got up and headed toward the shower. "You joining me?"

"Nah, I'mma go get the kids ready for chilling with daddy day," I replied while looking at her hips.

I knew I felt a little weight on her when she was riding my dick and her hips were really starting to spread. When she went and got in the shower to go handle her business, I got up and went to the office.

I walked over to her side and opened up her draw to pull out her calendar. Flipping through the pages, I was able to locate a red circle until I stopped at this month and there wasn't any. I calculated when she could have gotten pregnant and it would have been the day that I came home, however, I remembered her coming home smelling like the next nigga.

I just stood there in disbelief as I tried to make myself believe that the baby Lala was carrying was mine until the red light that indicated that she had a voicemail on her office phone started beeping.

Hello Lala this China from the Women's Clinic confirming your appointment for next week. I just wanted to let you know to not eat after midnight, to wear something comfortable, and to make sure you bring a driver with you. If you have any other questions feel free to give us a call back here at the clinic. Have a nice day.

The date on the voicemail indicated that her appointment was set for today. She knew she was pregnant and was on her way to abort the baby without telling me. Tears began to fall out of my eyes because the only reason she would be doing this behind my back was because in her heart she must have believed that the baby wasn't mine. The thought of someone else entering her garden and placing seeds in it made me weak to the knees.

Hearing Amire cry, I got up and went to go tend to him. Picking up my son, I took him to their bathroom so that I could change him and get him ready for our outing. I gave him a quick bath, dressed him in his Polo outfit, and made him a bottle.

When Amire was settled in his bouncer, Amiracle woke up crying. I took her to the bathroom got her cleaned up and dressed her in a pink Polo dress. I gave her a bottle and sat her in front of me, so that I could pull her hair out of her face. Taking the baby oil, I dabbed some in the palm of my hand and gently rubbed it in her hair. I used the brush to sweep all of her curly hair to the center of her head. Using the bow, I wrapped it up in a ponytail and placed a ribbon around it.

"Daddy got skills," I cooed and kissed her on her chubby cheeks. She took the bottle out of her mouth a squealed in delight.

"What did you do to my baby hair?" Lala laughed as she entered the room. She was dressed like Plain Jane in a pair of sweats, white t-shirt, and white Air Forces.

"I fixed it up. Stop hating on my skills."

"Hating boy bye!" she said waving me off.

I got up and placed baby girl next to Amire in her bouncer and turned on Yo Gabba Gabba to keep them occupied. I went downstairs to pack them some snacks for their baby bags.

"Ok, bae, I'm going over to Lisa's you guys have fun and I'll see y'all later," Lala said before kissing me on the lips as she made her way to the door.

"If you go have that abortion, the kids and I will not be here when you come back," I shouted out to her before she could open the door. I didn't hear a response, but I knew she was standing there with a shocked expression on her face.

"You might as well come in here so that you can tell me the truth," I said and grabbed the cooler for the kids' milk.

"What is there to talk about?" she replied and took a seat at the bar.

"How about the fact that you failed to tell me that you was pregnant and that you made an appointment to terminate the pregnancy?"

"You wouldn't understand," she whispered.

"How the fuck wouldn't I understand, Lala, I'm your fucking man! I notice every fucking thing about you. I know your period like the back of my hand! I know when you run out of pads because I'm usually the one picking you up some with a pint of Cookie Dough ice cream! Try again, Lala, for real and this time watch what you say before I bust you in your fucking mouth!"

"I don't know who fathered my child, Stacks! I don't know if this baby I am carrying belongs to you. That is why I wanted to abort it."

"So, why not tell me about it?"

"I was too ashamed. What was I going to say? Bae, I'm pregnant, but it might not be yours. How would you have taken the news, Stacks?"

"I would have been upset, but if there was a chance of me being a father to that baby, I would wake up every day feeling like I lost another child. It was hard for me to lose two fucking kids, Lala, I can't let you terminate this pregnancy and this could be my baby."

"But, what if it's not?"

"Then that's a bridge that'll we will have to cross."

"Would you leave me?"

"No, I wouldn't. Even if that baby in you wasn't biologically mine, I would still take care of it as if it was my own. What the fuck do I look like letting another nigga come up in my fucking house just because he have a baby by you!"

She just sat there looking at me unconvinced by my words. I just prayed that she didn't kill that baby because if she did, it was going to be a wrap for us. I needed Lala to learn how to trust me. I was a man of my word and I wasn't going to leave her for getting knocked up by some nigga that she was fucking with because she was under the impression that I was dead. I wasn't that type of nigga, and I also wasn't the type that was going to force her to kill a baby because there was a chance that it wasn't mine.

I finished packing the kids bag and gathered all their things to put in my truck. Once I had their car seats hooked in, I buckled them in, and pulled out of the driveway. I was going to come home and fuck Lala and if she didn't allow me to it would have been because she aborted the baby against my wishes and I was going to make good on my word and take my youngings and clear it on her ass.

I took my kids to the mall so that we could do some shopping. They were now eight months and starting to outgrow all of their clothes. I drop bands after bands on each store we went to buying nothing but the best for my shawtys. I even picked up a few things for Lala. Walking inside the Victoria Secret store, I was in search for something sexy for Lala to wear for me tonight. As I was looking at this black sheer see through negligee set, a woman approached me.

"Hey, are those your kids?"

"Yes." I smiled down at them.

"They are so cute!!" she gushed.

"Thank you."

"You buying that for me?" she flirted while pointing at the negligee set I held in my hand.

"Nah, for my wife."

"You're married?" she asked as she inspected my ring finger.

"Not yet, but I will be soon."

"In that case, I have a chance to prove to you why I should be wearing that for you tonight."

I laughed at this thot bitch that was standing in front of me. She was nowhere near my type. For one, she was all bones. I was a real man not a dog, so I needed some meat on my woman. I needed something to grab on when I was hitting it from the back. She looked like she would break if I tried to give her the dick.

"I'm good ma' wifey already earned her place in my heart, plus she blessed me with my babies ain't no way a bitch replacing her."

"Well, if you change your mind here's my number," She said and handed me a card. These hoes had no type of chill. Even when you tell a bitch the truth about you having a woman at home, they still be trying to throw the pussy at you.

I paid for the outfit then went to the Gucci store to find her a bad pair of pumps to wear with it. I was about to go to the bank and cash out and have her put on a show for a nigga. It'd been a minutes since she made that ass clap for me and now that it was now more fuller and juicer I wanted her to do a spilt on my face and make that ass jiggle.

I took the kids to Jump Zone, a little inflatable bounce house place that was located next to the mall. I watched them as they interacted and played with the other kids that were in the baby area. The smile on their little faces were priceless and these were the moments that I cherished the most.

I could only imagine my mother doing this on her own while she was raising me, that was why I made it my priority to spend quality time with just my kids and I. I never wanted them to feel as if their father was not there.

The kids started rubbing on their eyes and getting cranky. Looking down at my watch, I noticed that it was naptime. Picking them up, I carried them to the car and strapped them in. As I was putting the stroller in the trunk, I could have sworn there was an unmarked car parked in the far corner of the parking lot. I got in the car and made sure that the gun that I had registered in my name was under my seat. I just prayed no motherfuckers were bold enough to bring any heat my way while my youngins were in the car with me.

I started my ignition and began to pull off and that was when the unmarked car speed off. I tried to get the license plate number, but the driver drove off with so much speed that I couldn't. I wanted to follow the car, but my whining babies in the car changed my mind.

I made a mental note to double up security around my kids at all times. I was now sitting at the top of the ladder. Niggas needed me to eat. With that much power came with a boatload of haters that'll do anything to get at you even if they had to involve innocent children.

Stopping at Boston Market, I picked up dinner for Lala and I then headed home. I asked one of the guards to give me a hand carrying the sleeping babies inside. Placing them in their crib, I bent down and kissed both of their chubby cheeks before turning on the baby cameras I had installed.

Entering the master bedroom, I spotted Lala in the bed knocked out. She was dressed in the same thing only she was pants less and the way her ass was eating up them boy shorts had a nigga ready to bust one. I decided to let her get her rest because right after I fed her, I was going to put that ass to work.

Chapter 26

Joey

Sitting down at the Starbucks, I went over my case files on Stacks while waiting for Jimmy to join me. He had been under the FBI observation since he was back in Flint, but due to lack of evidence, they were never able to nail him.

Stacks was a very smart man. He never dealt directly with the dope so even when we did a few raids, we were never able to catch him. With all the surveillance and bugs I planted, I had enough information to bring Lala down, however, since Stacks was now back in the picture, she was no longer a priority.

"You needed my services detective?" Jimmy asked taking a seat across from me.

"Dear brother, long time no see."

"You ain't no brother of mine. Money talks, so what's up?"

"I have a few people I want you to check out for me."

"When you say check out, do you mean you want me to give you information on them?"

"Yes, you are a P.I. right?"

"I don't do the type of work you want done."

"What type of work do you do?"

"None of your fucking business pig!"

"Ouch! You still in your feeling over the death of your mother?"

"Fuck you! I should kill yo ass right now," he seethed. I could see the anger arise in his eyes.

"That would give you the death penalty."

"Suck my dick bitch!"

"I need you to look into these people for me, oh and I'll tell father you said hi," I said and slid the folder toward him and before getting out of my seat.

"Fuck you and that pussy nigga!

"Later solider," I laughed and walked out of the coffee shop.

It was very ironic how my father spoke so highly of Jimmy when he could care less about him. My father cheated on my mother and as a result, he ended up with Jimmy. My father paid Jimmy's mother off just so she'd keep quiet.

Eventually, she did and moved on with the neighborhood dope boy that was under investigation by my father at that time. She ended up pregnant again with her daughter and shortly after, my mother found out of my father's infidelities. Out for revenge one night, my mother cut the cords in their car in the attempt of killing all of them, but ended up only killing their mother and her boyfriend.

Being that my father was an officer of the law, he was able to cover it up for her and make it look like an accident. On the day of the funeral, my father and I went together where he decided it was finally time that we met. That day Jimmy made it clear that him and his little sister wanted nothing to do with us and that his real father was the man that was being buried along with his mother. My father always kept tabs on Jimmy and always made it his business to rub all of his accomplishments in my face.

When Jimmy decided to leave the coffee shop, I followed him. He stopped in front of Lisa's house and sat in the car. I figured since she was one of the people that I had in the file I gave him that he decided to start working. I sat there and watch him observe the house then make a few phone calls.

Thirty minutes of sitting there and watching him do nothing, I decided to drive off. I sent a copy of his license plate to one of the officers and had them put him on watch as well. I still had to figure out his ties to Ashley.

Lala: *Meet me at Joe's Crab Shack by the beach in fifteen minutes.*

I read the text from Lala and made an illegal U-Turn in the middle of the road to go meet her. She had an appointment with the abortion clinic a few days ago, so I wanted to know if she went through with killing my baby or not. I was at the point that I was about to have her ass arrested since she felt the need to ignore my calls.

I made it to the restaurant before Lala, so I took a seat at the bar and sent her a text to let her know where I was sitting. Flagging down a waitress, I placed an order for a side of coconut shrimp and a Corona. I was just about to pull out my phone and call Lala when someone took a seat next to me.

"Lala couldn't make it, but anything you can say to her can go through me," Stacks said removing the Fendi shades that probably cost more than my mortgage from his eyes.

"I think this is between Lala and I; no disrespect."

"Say what you have to say now because the next time you call my wife's phone, the next visit I make won't be a pleasant one."

"You threatening the wrong one."

"Partna' I don't make threats, I tell it like it is."

"Tell Lala to make sure my child is alive and well," I said purposely trying to hit a nerve.

"Your child," he laughed. "Nothing that comes out of my wife belongs to you. I suggest you lose her number and go about your business."

"We'll see."

"I'm done talking, try me." The waiter came and brought me my food. He went in his wallet and pulled out a gold money clip. Pealing off two fifty-dollar bills he dropped it on the table before walking away. I couldn't wait until I was able to bring down that cocky motherfucker.

Chapter 27

Lala

"Quit or the food is never going to get done," I said smacking Stacks on the arm as he tried to pry his fingers between my legs.

"Damn, ma, why that pussy gotta be so wet though?"

"Stop being nasty. I need to hurry up and finish the food."

Today we were throwing Anna a surprise birthday cookout at the park. We invited all of her family to come help us celebrate. For her birthday, we sent her to Hawaii and her flight was scheduled to land at three, so I had less than five hours to have everything prepared.

"Let me get a little taste," Stacks begged while licking on my weak spot.

"Nooo," I moaned as he pinned both of my hands up on the wall and pulled my dress up above my waist. He pulled my panties from the side and entered me with one thrust. I was still a little sore from the so called miscarriage that I had, plus I really didn't want to have sex until I went to the doctor for my follow up visit and got a depo-shot.

"You good?" Stacks whispered in my ears as he kept stroking me.

"Yesssss," I replied praying that he wouldn't nut inside of me.

It's not that I didn't want to have a baby again, I was just feeling guilty. The day after Stacks stopped me from getting an abortion, I called up the clinic and bought the abortion pill. I went through a series of cramps and started to bleed blood clots. When Stacks took me to the doctor, they ruled it as a miscarriage.

I hated to have to deceive Stacks, but I knew it wasn't going to work if the baby wasn't his. I felt in my heart our relationship was going to change for the worse. Right now, I just wanted to focus on the twins and working towards actually getting married; a baby wasn't meant for us to have at the moment anyways.

"SHIT!" Stacks yelled out as he dumped he seeds in me. I was low key mad that he didn't pull out, but I didn't let it show. I went to the bathroom and pushed all the nut out of me before hopping in the shower and cleaning off.

"You peeing out my nut is not going to prevent you from getting pregnant, I'm packing some heavy hitters," Stacks said as he entered the bathroom.

"How about I get on birth control?" I suggested.

"Why would you want to do that?"

"To prevent pregnancy."

"What's wrong with having my babies?"

"Nothing is wrong with it, it's just that the twins are still young and we still are not married."

"Is this what it's about?" he asked getting in the shower with me. "Is this about us not being married?"

"Yes. I mean, I want us to have kids as husband and wife so I know it's real."

"Lala, look at me. This is as real as it gets. Me marrying you is just some bullshit ass paper. As far as I'm concerned, you've been my wife."

"I want a wedding."

"Plan it ma, you already own my heart, I gave you the ring, so set a date and plan the wedding, I'll be there," he said and slid his dick in me from the back.

An hour and a sore pussy later, I was back in the kitchen finishing up the side dishes for the party. I made all of Anna's favorites which consisted of BBQ baked chicken, collard greens, potato salad, baked macaroni, Marconi salad, mixed veggies, rice, cabbage, green bean casserole, corn bread, pineapple upside down cake, sweet potato pie, and banana pudding. Covering all the dishes with foil paper, I laid them across the table so that Stacks could load up the car.

Once the food was loaded inside the car, we headed over to Tropical Park where the festivities were being held. I had the whole pavilion area rented and section offed as a private party. I would have rather rented out a nice banquet hall and had a nice party for Anna there, but she was so country that she enjoyed having a nice family BBQ instead. Lisa had the park beautifully decorated and Ralph was on the grill doing his thing. The DJ was just setting up his set and people should be pouring in any minute now.

"You did a great job chick," I complimented Lisa and then picked up Amire out of her hand. I placed sloppy kisses all over his plump, juicy cheeks making him laugh out loud.

"Your nasty ass is should have been here. I'm glad you finally decided to hop off the dick to join us," she laughed.

"Oh, shut up. It wasn't even like that. Do you see all that food I had to cook?"

"Boohoo, you should have had it catered."

"Now, you know Anna was not about to go for no catered food."

"I know that's right them country folks love them some greens and ham hocks," she joked.

How long has she been sleep?" I asked feeling on Amiracle's diaper.

"Twenty minutes now, that little diva is something else."

"You know Stacks the only one that can handle her spoiled butt."

"Speaking of the devil, here they come," Lisa said as she nodded her head toward Stacks and Ralph as they headed in our direction.

"It's time for you to go pick up Anna," I told Stacks.

"I'm on my way now. Where my little mama?"

"She sleep," I replied pointing at her as she peacefully slept in her portable crib.

"Iight then, Ralph you gon' be good?"

"Yeah, I'm straight bruh."

"I'll be back," Stacks said kissing me on the lips before leaving to go pick up Anna from the airport.

Anna's family started pouring into the park. Some of them I knew and others were introduced to me by her daughter.

"This is my brother Tarrio, but everyone calls him Tazz," Anna's daughter Tamika said as she introduced me to her brother that I had never met.

"Nice to meet you, Tazz."

"Likewise," he greeted and flashed me a smile filled with golds. Something about this cat didn't seem right, but I didn't want to ruin Anna's birthday party, so I just charged it to the game.

The party was now in full effect and all of her family members were here and they were showing out. For Anna to be so well mannered, her family was a bunch of ratchet folks. Her drunk cousin kept trying to hit on Ralph and it was so funny because Lisa was seconds away from pulling out the nine on her ass. I had to hold Lisa back a couple of times when she started to grab on Ralph's ass.

"Ms. Anna got some interesting family members," Lisa said as we watched the grandpa's old ass trying to do the Hot Nigga.

"Yeah, these some real country folks." My phone started beeping. I had two texts; one from Joey that I ignored and another from Stacks telling me that they were on their way.

"Everyone, Anna will be here shortly," I announced to the crowd of country folks. Tazz caught my attention. He was just lingering in the back not really doing anything. I caught him on the phone arguing with someone a few times, but other than that, he made no attempt to be around his family.

A bad feeling began to run through my body. I made sure that my gun was securely tucked in the small of my back. If anything was to go down, I was well prepared.

"Ok, everyone get in place," I said as I spotted Stacks walking over with a blindfolded Anna. I held my fingers up to count to three then everyone yelled out surprise. Stacks took off the blindfold and Anna stood there shocked to see all of her family members.

"Oh my God! Thank you!!" she exclaimed as she gave both Stacks and I hugs.

"You're welcome, Anna," I said kissing her on the cheeks. "I don't know what I'd do if it wasn't for you."

"Aww, thank you baby. You and those little ones mean so much to me. Speaking of babies, where are they? I missed them so much."

"They're over there in there… NOOOOOO!!!" I yelled and took off running toward the lady that was trying to walk off with my babies. I pulled out my gun and ran towards her full speed. I aimed my gun and left off two shots.

POW!! POW!!

I was able to hit her in the shoulder, which slowed her down a bit.

POW! POW! POW!

I heard more gunshots as I tried to run, but my body started to slow down. I kept trying to tell my legs to move and go run after the bitch that had my babies, but the wouldn't cooperate. Everything started to move slowly around me as I heard more gunshots and saw blurry shadows run past me.

"LALA!!?" I heard someone call out my name. I tried to respond, but my mouth wouldn't move. I struggled to keep my eyes open, but my eyelids were getting heavy. The last thing I was able to see before everything went black was Tazz's face. My gut told me he had something to do with my babies disappearing.

Chapter 28

Ashley

Being able to finally kill Lala made my pussy drip in excitement. I made sure to shoot her in the stomach a few times just to ensure that the bastard child that she was carrying for Joey was dead. I was so pissed when I learned that she was pregnant from him that I contemplated on killing his ass, too.

Here he was telling me that he wasn't ready to have another baby, but he was basically begging her to keep hers. I didn't know what was so good about Lala that kept the niggas going crazy and now that she was dead, I didn't care to find out.

I paid my one of my home girls, Bebe, from the projects to keep an eye on the twins for me. I wasn't going to really take them, but when I found out Stacks was really alive, I decided that I could get paid. This time

I had to make sure that I had the right people on my team in order for me to successfully pull this off.

I had my cousin Red and his homeboy Tazz helping me, but in order for all of us to stay alive, I needed a stronger team. We were all trying to become millionaires and live long enough to spend the money.

"Hey, Bebe, how's the babies?" I asked while walking around the new three-bedroom apartment I moved her into.

"The little boy is a good baby, but that little girl is a damn devil all she do is cry and shit," she said waving one of her long stiletto fingernails in the air. I went in their room and watched them as they sleep. I had to admit Lala and Stacks made some beautiful children. It was unfortunate that they would have to grow up without a mother.

"When you gon' give me the rest of my money?" she asked while popping her gum.

"When I get it, then it's yours. I pay your bills for you; I buy the kids everything that they need, what the hell you need money for? I'm paying your ass to just sit here and watch these kids, this is way better than selling your ass for a hair do don't you think?"

"Whatever, but a bitch got a life, too. I want to go to the club shit!"

"I'll come by this weekend to keep an eye on the kids, so that you could go out."

"Shit that's all I ask, and a new outfit."

"You pushing it."

"Bitch, you owe me. I could go to jail for this little shit that you pulling."

"Ok, damn, I'll bring you some money to go get you an outfit." I rolled my eyes. I hated doing business with ghetto bitches.

"Good!"

"I'll come back and check on them later. Don't let no one in this house and don't leave with them either. If they need anything call me," I instructed.

"I know girl dang, you ain't gotta keep talking to me like I'm a child."

"Whatever, lock the door when I leave," I said and walked out of the house and got into my car.

I got in my car and strapped my seatbelt.

"Oh, shit!" I yelled out in pain as I hit where Lala shot me. It was so hard trying to hide it from Joey, especially since he was a detective and he could spot a bullet wound from a mile away. *Speak of the devil;* I thought as my phone began to ring and his name flashed across the screen.

"Sup bae," I purred in to the phone.

"Hey, where are you? I have to get back to the station."

"Damn, Joey, all I ask for is one day to myself and for you to watch our son!" I yelled I was starting to become real sick and tired of becoming number two to his damn job.

"I know, but something has come up."

"What is that?"

"A new lead on this very important case that I'm working on."

"Yeah, whatever, Joey, I'll be home in a few," I said and hung up the phone without saying goodbye.

When I got home, Joey was in the bathroom taking a shower and my son was in our bed sleeping. I quickly packed his book bag and grabbed his car seat and put them both in the car. I went to his phone and turned on the GPS tracker, then scrolled through his messages.

There wasn't anything unusual there, so I went through his email. An open email between him and his father was already open and on display. I screenshot it and quickly sent it to my phone before deleting the evidence. Placing his phone back, I walked out of the room and sat at the table to read the email.

Joey: *I got the information on Lisa.*

Dad: *Ok and?*

Joey: *Before I proceed, why were you so determined that I check her out?*

Dad: *If you did your research correctly you would know why.*

Joey: *Did you know about Jimmy, too?*

Dad: *That he was a contract killer? Yes, I knew.*

Joey: *Ok, again what was your purpose?*

Dad: *When you take Lala and Stacks down I want her to be....*

"I didn't hear you come in." Joey scared me causing me to drop my phone on the floor.

"Yes, I been here."

"I see that Kindle app took up all of your attention."

"Yes these books seem so real, I get caught up all in these character's drama."

"I see. Well, I'm out of here. I'm going to try to make it home by dinner."

"Ok, see you later bae," I said and kissed him on the lips.

I waited until I heard his car door shut before going in the room and grabbing my son. He started to cry because he was still sleepy, so I patted him on the back. Placing him in his car seat, I buckled him in. I turned on the GPS system in my car then used bluetooth to sync his location. I waited for the information to load up before I pulled off.

As the lady directed me to his location, my mind went back to the email. I knew Lisa and Joey were brother and sister, but what did that have to do with Jimmy? Was Joey still working on the Lala and Stacks' case? I had a lot of unanswered questions that were bound to get answered today.

Chapter 29

Stacks

My head was all the way fucked up. My kids were missing and I was sitting here next to my wife waiting for her to wake up. I thanked God that I didn't lose her. I didn't know what I would do if I ever had to live my life without her. My head started killing me, so I went outside to smoke a blunt in my car. I informed the nurses that I was going to step out for a brief second and to call me on my cell if she woke up.

Grabbing the pound of Kush out of my glove compartment, I took some out and began breaking it down with my fingers. I was trying to think long and hard on who I could have been beefing with, but I came up empty.

I needed Lala to wake up, so that I could ask her if she knew anyone that may have been gunning for her. The thought of someone fucking with my kids made me mad enough to flip this whole city over.

Sealing my blunt closed; I lit it and took a long pull. Blunt after blunt, I hot boxed my car while jamming Migos' *First 48*. I tried to collect my thoughts, but the thoughts of my shawtys out there with someone that was most likely beefing with me kept fucking my head up. Just as I was about to get out of my car and head back in the hospital, a cop decided to pull up behind me.

"Fuck!"

I thought as I watched him walk towards my car and tap on my window. I sent Ralph a quick text to call my lawyer and let him know to wait by the phone for my call. The minute I rolled down my window, a cloud of smoke smacked the officer right in the face.

"How can I help you officer?"

"Sir, I'm going to have to ask you to step out of the car."

"What seems to be the problem officer?"

"I am going to ask you one more time to step out of the car," he said and pulled out his radio and called for backup. I knew I was going to go to jail. I had Kush all in my car; there was no way around it.

Within seconds, the parking lot was flooded with pigs and their fucking dogs. The amount of officers that came out you would have thought I was a terrorist or some shit. The fat pig reached in my car, pulled me out, and punched me in my mouth.

I smiled at him as I spit the blood out that was filling up in my mouth on the ground purposely getting some on his shoes. This enraged him and he started kicking me. I felt my rib cage crack as he continued to kick me until one of the officers grabbed him off of me. The way he was on me you would have thought we had a personal vendetta against one another.

I made sure to get his badge number. Just because he was working for the law didn't mean his ass was untouchable. I was about to do more damage to him than he thought he did to me. Yeah, I was hurt but all they dumb ass ended up doing was giving my lawyer a reason to have my case thrown out.

When I made it to the Dade County Correctional Department, they refused to give me my phone call or even call my lawyer. Even though I never really got tied up in the law, the first thing I did when I moved to Miami was research the best criminal defense attorney Miami had to offer. David M. Edlestein was the best. His win rate was higher than every lawyer in the state of Florida.

I sat in this cold ass cell with no toilet for four hours according to the clock that was hung on the hallway wall. My ribs were killing me, I had blood all over my shirt, and not once had anyone came to give me some medical treatment.

I was starting to get so fucking frustrated that I dropped to the floor and started doing push ups to kill time. The sharp pain from my ribs were excruciating. Biting on my bottom lip, I sucked in the pain and continued relieving my stress. I was on push up number two hundred when I heard my lawyer's voice demanding that I get released.

Sitting up on the floor, I removed my shirt and used it to wipe the sweat off of my face. I heard keys jiggling then the cell doors unlocked.

"Look at my client. He looks in need of medical attention," David snapped. "I can't wait to see the mayor's face when I bring this to his attention. This is going to make great press."

"Jones you're free to go, on behalf of the Miami Dade Police Department, I would like to apologize."

"Get out my face," I said as I got up and walked out of the cell.

"This is not over yet," my lawyer threatened before following behind me.

"Do you need to go to the hospital?" David asked as soon as we got outside.

"Yes, take me to the University of Miami Hospital."

"Hop in." I got in his all black BMW four series, reclined my seat back, and allowed my body to sink in the soft, pecan colored interior.

"Call me if those assholes decide to fuck with you again," David said upon pulling up to the front entrance of the hospital.

"Thank, D, good looking out."

"One phone call away," he replied before pulling off.

Walking to the hospital, I wasn't interested in seeking medical attention. I had to check on Lala and make sure she was good. I spotted Lisa coming out of her room, so I flagged her down.

"How's she doing?"

"Where the hell you been? You looked like you was jumped."

"Them fucking pigs tried to fuck with me in the parking lot. Is Lala good?"

"Yeah, she's good, she ain't wake up yet. The doctor was asking for you. Go have a seat with her and I tell him that you're here."

"Iight."

I winced in pain as I took a seat in the chair next to Lala's bed. I reached in my pockets for my phone, but then I remembered that I left it in my car. I had to make sure that they didn't fuck around and tow my shit. Most likely knowing those nasty fuckers they probably did.

"Hey Mr. Jones, I was looking everywhere for you," the doctor said as he walked inside of the room.

"I had to run a quick errand, but I'm back now. How is Lala?"

"I have some good news and some bad news."

"Good news is that Lala is perfectly fine. We were able to remove all of the bullets with no problem."

"The bad news?"

"The bad news is the bullet that pierced her abdomen, scarred some tissue that was being healed which may cause some complication with her trying to get pregnant in the future."

"I'm not following."

"Did Lala recently have an abortion?"

"No, but she had a miscarriage."

"When we performed an x-ray, we saw a lot of tissue that were healing, which usually occurs when a baby is forced out of the womb."

"So, you're trying to say that she had an abortion?"

"That's what it looks like."

"Will she be able to have kids in the future?"

"It is very much possible in the future, but right now no. Not until the tissue has fully healed."

"Is that all doc?" I asked feeling my body temperature rise.

"Lala is also going to need therapy in order for her to walk normally with her right leg."

"Why?"

"The bullet tore through her abdomen and hit a muscle in her leg, which we had to perform surgery on to repair. Before she goes home, we're going to put a boot on her leg just to help the muscles heal a little faster, but she will need some therapy. Other than that, everything is fine. We lowered her dose of morphine, so she should be waking up soon."

"Thank you doctor."

"No, problem. I'll be back to check on her later. You should really get checked out, you don't look too good," he said before walking out of the room.

Unable to sit with Lala anymore, I got up and checked myself into the emergency room. They did a few X-rays that determined that I had some fractured ribs. I called Ralph on the hospital phone and told him to pick me up.

After the nurse dressed my rib cage, I had her fax all of my hospital paperwork to my lawyer's office. I was going to have my lawyer hit their ass with a big lawsuit. Not that I needed their money, I had more than enough money to have the whole department on my payroll. I just wanted to fuck with them the same way they had came and fucked with me.

The Doctor suggested that I stay overnight, but I declined and discharged myself. I made sure that I gave Lala's nurse instructions to call me as soon as she woke up. I had to really talk to her to see what she was thinking. I forbade her from getting rid of the baby. I told her that our relationship was on the line if she did it, and she turned around and did it any way. Then she lied about it by trying to cover it up with some damn miscarriage.

I didn't know who the fuck she turned into, but she was not the woman I fell in love with. The thug life that she temporarily lived while I was gone must have gotten to her because she was smelling herself.

"What's up bruh," Ralph greeted me when I got in the car.

"Nothing nigga just stressing. The streets ain't saying shit about my seeds?"

"Nah, nobody coming forward."

"Shit man. Lala wasn't beefing with nobody?"

"Except for that Carla shit, nah."

I thought for a quick second that it could probably be Carla behind the kidnapping of my kids, but what was their motive? I handled that situation and I made sure everyone was being fed and full.

"You think it was them?" Ralph asked.

"Nah, but I'm not putting shit past nobody. I'mma check that out. Keep your ears to the streets and make sure you let motherfuckers know I'm willing to pay top dollar for the safe return of my kids."

"I got you. Lala straight?"

"Yeah, she good. Get one of them lil niggas to swing by the impound lot to pick up my whip," I said and got out the car

"Iight kid holla at you later."

Dapping the security guards up, I made my way in the house. The inside of my house felt so cold and lonely. There were no cries from my babies. I wasn't greeted by the scent of Lala's perfume, or smile.

Sitting at my desk in the office, I pulled out a bottle of Hennessy and started sipping. I made arrangements to have a personal therapist come to the house and help Lala with her therapy. I also asked Anna if she was able to come stay over with Lala for a few days until she was able to manage on her own.

After making all of the arrangements, I hired a cleaning company to come by tomorrow and clean the whole house from top to bottom. I wanted to make everything as comfortable as possible for Lala when she returned home.

I booked the penthouse suit at the Ritz Carlton then went upstairs to pack my things. I wasn't about to play these types of games with Lala. She knew what was up when I gave her my ultimatum, but she decided to go behind my back and do exactly what I told her not to do.

Now, I had three kids that I lost by the hands of someone who intentionally wanted to take them away from me. This was an unforgivable act and at the moment I wasn't even sure if I wanted to be with her sneaky ass anymore.

Chapter 30

Joey

I sat at my desk and waited for my dad to come from his meeting with the mayor. I knew he was going to tear me a new asshole. I was acting off of impulse and allowed my emotions to cloud my judgment. Since the day Stacks disrespected me at Joe's, I'd been looking for ways to make his life a living hell. My men were supposed to inflict pain, make him suffer, but still follow the police protocol.

They failed to do so many things, most importantly when they arrested him; they forgot to read him his Miranda rights. He was beaten and not given any medical treatment and all of his request to speak with his lawyer were all denied. I was pissed at them for being so damn sloppy.

My father walked inside my office with his face screwed up. He slammed the door behind him and stood there giving me an evil glare.

"Where the fuck did I go wrong with you?" he rhetorically asked. "How the fuck did you manage to fuck up this bad?!"

"Dad…"

"Don't fucking dad me! You are suspended without pay! Turn in your badge and gun please."

"Let me explain."

"There isn't shit that you can say that can fix the fact that I have a thirty million dollar lawsuit sitting on my desk! I don't know why I ever decided to give you this case."

"Stacks will be the biggest bust yet. If we take him down, this could fix everything."

"I said no! Stacks is not to be touched anymore! This investigation is closed. When you return from your suspension, you will be on office duty until I decide you are capable of doing your job correctly. Now, get the fuck out of my precinct."

Handing my father my badge and gun, I gathered my paperwork and left the station. If he thought this was going to stop me from fucking Stacks' life up then, he had another thing coming. Even if I wasn't able to bring him down, I had enough power to eliminate his ass.

Picking up my phone, I called my brother Jimmy and told him that we had to put our differences aside because I was in need of his services. I set up a meeting with him then went to the bank to withdraw the money that he was requesting upfront.

Chapter 31

Lala

I woke up to a whole bunch of beeping sounds. Looking around, I could see cords and tubes all over my body. The last thing I remembered was my babies and then Tazz. Wait a minute, my babies. Where were they? I tried to speak up and say something, but my throat was to dry. Locating the call button, I repeatedly pushed it until a nurse came into my room.

"Hello, Ms. Williams, nice of you to finally join us. Let me go grab the doctor and I'll be right back," the nurse said and left the room. A few minutes later, a male doctor came in the room and removed the tubes that they had down my throat. The nurse brought me a cup of ice-cold water that I quickly gulped down. I pointed for her to pour me another cup that I gulped down, as well.

"Where are my babies?" I whispered still felling the rawness in my throat.

"What babies?" the doctor asked confused.

"My twins," I hysterically began to cry.

"It's ok, Doc, I got it from here," I heard Lisa's voice say as she walked in the room and wrapped her arms around me.

"I'll be back later to check on you. If you need anything contact your nurse," The doctor said and left the room.

"Lisa, where are my babies?" I asked in a childlike voice.

"Stacks is still out there looking for them. He's going to find them," she assured me as she rocked me back and forth. Lisa began to softly rub my back as I cried. The motion of her rocking me back and forth was enough to put me asleep again.

***

Three days of observation, I was finally released from the hospital. I knew Stacks was putting in overtime trying to find our kids that was why I didn't trip too much when he didn't come visit me. I wasn't really able to walk, so I had to use crutches to get around. Lisa coming to pick me up from the hospital and not Stacks had me feeling some type of way. Not really wanting to talk about it, I just shut my mouth and tried my best to enjoy the ride home.

Anna met us at the door and helped Lisa carry my things in the house. All of my things were arranged in the guest bedroom that we had on the first level to avoid me having to go up and down the elevator.

I sent Stacks my fourth text message asking him where he was when Anna walked in the room with a bowl of homemade beef stew. It was one of my favorite meals, but I had no appetite to eat.

"Lala, I know you miss those babies, and I do too, but you have to eat. You don't want them babies coming home scared of you because you look like a pile of bones."

"Where's Stacks?"

"He's out looking for them babies, leave that man alone. Men are different from us females. When we're going through something, we like to have an entourage, but when men are hurting, they like to do it in peace. He'll be home."

"Could you please grab me two Aleves? I have a terrible headache"

"Yes, as soon as you eat. That's probably why you have the headache."

I took a few sips of the stew then took the two Aleves. I grabbed a picture of my babies that was on the nightstand and cried myself to sleep.

"Lala." I looked up and saw Stacks sitting on the edge of the bed gently shaking me awake.

"Where have you been?"

"I've been trying to look for the twins. Do you have any information that could help me?"

"It was Tazz."

"Tazz?"

"Yes, Tazz," I said thinking back to that horrible day. "Tavion. Oh, my God, that's Anna's son."

"Wait, are you sure?"

"Yes, her daughter introduced me to him."

"Ms. Anna?" Stacks yelled out.

"Yes baby?"

"I have to ask you a question?"

"I'm listening."

"Do you have a son name Tazz?"

"Who Tavion?"

"Yes, ma'am."

"Yes. Tavion is my adopted son, but I haven't heard from him in months. He contacted me searching for money, but I refused to help him. He has always been a troubled child. Lord knows I love my babies, but I was happy when he finally turned eighteen."

"Do you know his whereabouts?"

"No. Why?"

"Lala believes that he may have something to do with the babies disappearing."

"Oh, God no! My adopted daughter, his biological sister still keeps in contact with him. I'll give you her number and you can see if that helps."

"Thank you very much, Anna."

"Anything that can help bring my babies home. I'll be in the front room knitting my babies some hats if you need me," she said and walked out of the room.

"The therapist should be here tomorrow."

"Where you going?"

"Back to a hotel?"

"Why are you in a hotel?"

"Lala, you lied to me."

"Lied to you about what?"

"The fucking baby that's what! You killed a baby that could have been mine and then lied about it. I would have respected you if you would have kept it one hundred, but now I don't know if I can even trust your sneaky ass. You went through a lot of work just to get rid of a baby that I gave my word to be in its life even if it wasn't mine. Then you sit up in the hospital boohoo crying and putting on a fucking show when you knew you purposely got rid of my baby!"

"Stacks, let me explain," I began to cry.

"Go ahead."

"I didn't want to burden you with a child that didn't belong to you. This was a very messy situation for me that I didn't feel comfortable in. This was only going to cause a whirlwind of trouble that I wanted to avoid."

"Don't give me that bullshit, Lala. I'm a stand up guy. There was no way in hell I was going to leave you."

"I'm sorry."

"Don't be, what's done is done. I'm out."

"Please don't go."

"I have to. I'm sick of looking at your snake ass!"

"So, just like that, we're done?"

"You knew what it was before you even made this decision," he said and walked out the door.

My heart began to feel real heavy. First, my kids were missing now my relationship was falling apart I didn't mean for things to go this far. I made the decision to terminate my pregnancy because I was thinking of the future of my family and I didn't want Joey fucking up our happy home.

Lying back in bed, I said a prayer for the safe return of my children. Pulling the comforter over my head I screamed at the top of my lungs and began crying my heart out.

Chapter 32

Ralph

"Do you really have to leave tomorrow?" Kandi asked me as we sat in Elven Madison Park and had dinner.

"Yes, I have to go home. I have to get back to the money."

"Well, the baby and I really enjoyed the few days you were able to come out and visit us."

"No problem. I wasn't about to miss my youngin first official doctor's appointment no way," I said taking a bite out of my cheesesteak.

"I'm going to be done with school before the baby is done. I'm thinking about living up here permanently.

"Word?"

"Yeah. This city is filled with opportunities for an upcoming fashion designer as myself," she laughed.

"Well, what about the baby?"

"I'll work something out."

"What about the plan of opening a boutique in Miami?" I asked trying to convince her to move back home. It was not that I wanted to be with her, I just didn't want to have to travel back and forth just to see my kid.

"I have to have the money for that first."

"Why you insulting me ma'?"

"What you mean?"

"It means if I got it, you got it. If you not having enough money to start up your business is what's stopping you then, I'm willing to give you the money.

"Why?"

"Because you are the mother of my child. If you're doing good then that means he or she will always be straight."

"Thank you very much!" she squealed as she jumped out of her seat and onto my lap. She started kissing me all over my face and slipped her tongue in my mouth. I just sat there and allowed her to have her way with my mouth.

"How's your relationship with Lisa?" she asked.

"We're working on it?"

"What about what we talked about?"

"Just chill," I cut her off not wanting to have that conversation with her.

I was trying my hardest to be cordial with her so she wouldn't turn into a baby mama from hell, but she was making it too damn hard. Her feelings were so involved that no matter how much I was there that would never be enough. She wouldn't be satisfied unless we were in a relationship.

Signaling the waitress for the check, I paid it then, we left to go maternity shopping. Kandi wasn't even showing yet, so I had no clue as to why she wanted to maternity shop so soon. I knew this was just another one of her little tricks to get me to spend more time with her, so I just went along with it.

Nothing I paid for came from a maternity store, nor did she buy anything in a bigger size. Shaking my head, I continued to drop bands after bands on her until she was tired and hungry again.

Making a quick run to the Jamaican spot to grab her the curry chicken she was so badly craving, we finally made it to her house. As I was carrying the last of her bags in the house, my phone started to ring. Glancing at the screen, I saw Lisa's name flashing across. I placed all of her bags on her bed and went outside to answer my phone.

"Sup sexy."

"When are you coming home?" she replied.

"Why you missing daddy's dick?"

"Nah I'm missing daddy's face!" she laughed.

"I'm tying up these last few loose strings for Stacks. My flight touchdown in the A.M, you scooping me up?"

"Text me the information and I'll think about it."

"Man stop playing. I expect to see your ass there in a mini dress with no panties on."

"Boy bye!"

"I love you too, night bae."

"Good night, Ralph," she said and hug up the phone.

I was finally able to get her to have a conversation with me, there was no way in hell I was telling her that I came to New York to spend time with Kandi. Lisa had zero type of understanding and it would be like pulling teeth trying to get her to understand.

Lisa's way of thinking was for me to cease all contact with Kandi until a DNA test confirmed that it was my baby. My logic was a happy baby mama makes for a happy life and if there was a way for me to make Kandi happy without having to be in a relationship with her, I was going to do it.

"You done talking to your bitch?" Kandi asked as she came outside in a pink satin robe.

"Why she gotta be all that?"

"Because I don't like her."

"You don't even know her not to like her."

"I know she's the reason why our baby will never get to experience a two parent home and for that I can't stand her ass."

"I'm going to always be in my baby's life no matter who I'm with."

"That's not the point I'm trying to make. You grew up with just your mom. I know you always wondered how it would feel to have your father. I just wouldn't want our baby to feel that way." She began crying. Ever since Kandi got pregnant she became a hormonal wreck.

"That will never happen. As long as I'm alive, my child will never want to know how it feels to have a father because I am going to make it my business to always be there. We don't have to be together to co-parent."

"I don't want to co-parent though. I want to be a family."

"Shhhh, ma don't cry, everything is going to work out."

"You promise."

"Ma trust me, I gotchu. Now, let's go inside, so that I can rub them ugly feet.

"My feet are not ugly." She laughed while hitting me on the chest.

Laying her down on her sofa, I grabbed the peach mango body oil and poured some in the palm of my hands. Rubbing the oil in my hand, I grabbed her feet and began rubbing them. I wasn't in the mood to give her dick, so I planned on rubbing her feet until she fell asleep.

Twenty minutes into the foot rub, she was knocked out and softly snoring. I carried her to her room and placed her in bed pulling the comforter over her body. Grabbing a pillow and a blanket off the bed, I went to the living room and fell asleep on the sofa.

I was awakened in the middle of the night by the sounds of slurping and pleasure shooting through my body. Looking down, I saw Kandi on her knees giving me some of her fye head. I used her head and guided her so that she was sucking on the spots that made my toes curl. After busting down her throat, I bent her over the arm of the couch and fucked her until it was time for me to get ready for my flight back home.

Chapter 33

Lala

"Up. Down. Up. Down. Up. Down. Up. Down," my physical therapist instructed as we did my legs exercises in the pool. This was my last week of therapy and I was glad because this bitch was starting to get a little too friendly with Stacks. She tried to get him to bring her home one night because her so called ride wasn't picking up the phone, but I shut that shit down quickly by suggesting that Anna bring her.

I really didn't see the need of her visits anyways. The boot was off of my leg and I was walking normally except for the slight limp that I had that the doctor assured would go away with time.

It had been three weeks since the day I got shot and the day my babies disappeared. No matter how many bodies Stacks went through, no one had no information on where my babies could be. Today made them nine months and instead of putting the cute little nine months sticker on their chest and taking cute little pictures of them for their keepsake box, I was stuck here in my feelings. It was as if this Tazz character and my kids fell off the face of the earth because they were nowhere to be found.

"Ok, Lala that is all for today. You are healing very quickly. Only a few more days left and you'll be done with therapy," she said getting out of the indoor pool that we had built in our pool house.

"That's good."

"Well, I'm about to get going before my ride have a fit. Tell Stacks I said hi."

"Ok," I replied really wanting to wrap my hand around the bitch throat and squeeze the life out of her ass. It was like she knew Stacks and I were no longer together and was trying to throw that shit in my face on the sly.

"Lala, your clinic is on your office phone," Anna yelled from the kitchen.

"Send the call to my cell phone."

"Hello," I answered.

"Lala, you need to get here quick!"

"Shelly, what's going on?"

"With all due respect, could you hurry up and get here it's important, please?" Shelly said before hanging up the phone.

I jumped up went to my closet and threw on a pair of jeans, a plain black t-shirt, and a pair of black Timberland boots. Pulling my hair in a high messy bun, I grabbed my keys and wallet and was out the door.

Hitting the alarm on my Range, I pulled out of the parking garage and headed toward my clinic. When I got there, police officers were everywhere. My heart started to pound in my chest as I hopped out my car and rushed to the front to see what's going on.

"Oh, my God, Lala. I tried to help them. I just saw them here, who would do that?" She began crying hysterically.

"Ma'am, are you Lala Williams?" the officer asked.

"Y-y-y-yes why?" I stuttered.

"Can you walk with me please?" I followed the officer away from all the madness that was going on to a quiet location.

"Do you have pictures of the twins that you reported missing?"

"Yes, um yes, I do, but um, why?" I asked feeling myself about to have a panic attack.

"May I please see the pictures?"

"Yes." I reached in my purse with my hands trembling. I pulled out the most recent picture of the twins and showed it to the officer.

"We have them."

"You do?" I asked. "Where?"

"Miami Children Hospital."

"Wait, why are they in the hospital."

"Ma'am, I advise you to go down there and see the condition that your kids are in. An officer will be there shortly to take your statement."

I ran to my car and made my way to the hospital. On my way there, I kept trying to call Stacks, but he wasn't answering my calls. Tears began to flood my eyes as I began to think the worst. Calming myself down, I asked God to watch over my babies for them and to allow them to be ok.

"Hi, may I help you?" the lady at the front desk lady asked.

"I'm looking for my twins Amire Anthony Jones and Amiracle Aniya Jones they were brought in today."

"May I please have their socials?"

I read off each of the kids' social security numbers to the lady as she typed something into the computer.

"One of the twins Amire is in room twenty four, however Amiracle is in our ICU unit."

"ICU? For what?" I asked beginning to panic.

"I'm not sure, you will have to talk to the doctor,"

I was able to go in the room and sit with Amire, but I had to speak with a doctor before going back to see Amiracle. My heart broke seeing my baby boy lay down in the small, little hospital bed looking so defenseless. I bent down to kiss his little chubby cheeks and noticed that they were burning up. I was about to go call a nurse until the doctor came in.

"Are you the twins' mother?"

"Yes."

"Both of the twins were found in front of your clinic burning a very high fever and with Pneumonia. Amiracle is in ICU because due to the fever, she kept having seizures. We were able to get Amire's fever under control, but for some reason her fever seems to rise higher and higher. We had to put her in a coma just to stop her body from having any more seizures and having and permanent damage done.

"Oh, God," I cried out. "Who would do this to my babies?"

"A sick person, whoever is behind this should be sitting under a jail cell. I'll let you sit and visit with

Amire when you're ready to see Amiracle just let the front desk nurse know and she'll bring you back."

"Thank you Doc."

"Try not to worry, your kids are some fighters and they will get through this."

Picking Amire up out of the crib, I was careful enough not to disturb any of the cords that he had hooked to his little body. I sat in the rocking chair with him in my lap and began rocking with him while singing him lullabies. His little eyes fluttered open and he looked at me and gave me a weak smile.

I kissed his chubby cheeks, laid him across my shoulders, and continued to rock him. When the nurse came to check his vitals, I decided to go check on my baby girl.

Scrubbing my hands and putting on the hair net and gown they provided me with, I walked over to the bed she was laying in. It broke my heart to see my princess in this position. I was seeing red and ready for blood.

Whoever decided to do this to my kids was going to pay the ultimate price for violating. I stayed with my kids alternating between sitting with both of them until visiting hours were over. I was able to bribe a nurse that allowed me to spend the night with Amire.

The next morning I woke up, my phone was dead, and I was in serious need of a toothbrush. I wanted to wait until the doctor did his rounds before going home and showering. I watched as the nurse checked Amire's vitals. Amire was now up and alert, but he was still weak. I played with the curly locks he had while he watched Nick Jr.

"Good morning, Lala."

"Good morning, Doc." I replied.

"Looks who's up. Hey buddy," the doctor said playing with Amire while checking him out at the same time.

"Amire looks fine, he's just a little dehydrated, but he is going to be ok. Our main concern is on Amiracle. I don't want to wake her up and risk her having another seizure."

"What do you suggest?" I asked.

"Well, we're going to give her a low dose of Phenobarbital then, wake her up if she does happen to have a seizure then it won't be hard for us to put her back to sleep."

"I'm trusting that you will do whatever you have to do to make sure that my daughter gets well."

"Yes you are at the best children hospital Miami has to offer we are going to make sure she get through this."

After making promises to come back and see them, I left and went home. When I walked through the door, Stacks was instantly on my trail bombarding me with questions.

"Answer me, Lala, where the fuck were you all night!"

"If you would have stop being a little bitch and answered when I called you, you would have known."

WHAM!

Stacks smacked my in the mouth instantly splitting my lip.

"Watch you fucking mouth when you talking to me!"

"Stacks, why are you here in my business? You moved out and made it clear that we were not together!" I said taking off my boots.

"Lala, I'm not about to argue with you. Your slick mouth gon' cause me to fuck you up!"

"Yeah, whatever."

"Fuck it I'm out!"

"Make sure you stop by Miami Children Hospital to go check on your kids."

"What did you say?" he asked and turned around.

"You heard what I said now go check on your babies."

"How did you find them?"

"Don't worry about it, just go see about your kids!"

He looked at me as if he was going to say something, but decided not to. I heard the door slam and the ignition of his car start. I watched him on the security system as he pulled off.

I called Lisa, but there was no answer, so I left her a voicemail telling her that her Godchildren were found and they were at the hospital. Not wanting to be away from my kids any longer, I packed me a duffle bags of things that I was going to need. I was prepared to pay whatever it cost to stay with my kids until they were released from the hospital. Double checking my bag for everything, I entered the hot, steamy shower and allowed the beads of the water to beat down on my tense skin.

Quickly showering, I got dressed to head back to the hospital. I grabbed my daughter her favorite bunny bear and headed towards my car. Since today was Anna's day off, I sent her a text to let her know what was going on.

When I got to the hospital, the whole crew was there except Stacks. My babies needed me, so I was not about to stress over his ass.

"Hey, Lala," Lisa said handing me a now very active Amire.

"Any word on baby girl?" I asked cradling Amire in my arms.

"Stacks is in ICU with her she's doing much better she's up now."

"No more seizures?"

"No, they were able to control it and her fever. They want her to finish up her antibiotics before bringing her in a regular room."

"Thank you Jesus!" I cried out happy to hear the good news.

Everyone sat around and hung out with the twins until visiting hours were over. Stacks was able to get the doctor to allow me to stay with Amire. Since ICU was closed and was not allowing any more visitors, he came down to play with Amire.

We didn't speak or make any type of eye contact. I really wanted to cry, but I didn't want him to see that the little act that he was putting on was affecting me. He played with Amire until his phone started beeping off the hook. I wanted to ask him who was blowing him up, but it was no longer my place. Without a goodbye, he left the room as if I didn't exist.

***

After a two-week stay in the hospital, the twins were finally cleared to come home. Stacks came and helped me bring them home. He stayed with them until they fell asleep and then left. I wasn't really sweating him. I was happy to have my babies back home.

I gave Anna the rest of the week off so that I could spend time with the babies, but that didn't stop her from coming over and taking care of them. I was in the kitchen cooking breakfast for Anna, the kids and I, when Stacks sent me a text telling me that he was having an emergency meeting at the headquarters and he wanted everyone present even Lisa and I.

I fed the kids their breakfast, gave them their bath, and played with them until they fell asleep for their nap.

"Anna, I know gave you the week off, but do you mind staying with the kids for me?" I asked picking up the toys that were thrown all over the family room floor.

"No, problem at all go ahead chile."

"Thank you."

I went upstairs and took a nice long bubble bath while sipping on a cup of wine and huffing on a fat blunt. Grabbing my wildberry body lotion, I moisturized my skin from head to toe. I decided to dress to kill as I laid my cream Gucci pants suit on the bed. I went in the bathroom and flat ironed my hair so that it was flowing straight down my back.

I applied light makeup to my face making sure to add an extra coating of the nude lipstick to my lips making them look nice and full. Dressed in my pants suit I slipped my feet in my cream colored Gucci pumps and grabbed my matching shades out of my accessory display box.

Color coordinating with my car, I decided to push my cream colored Lexus coupe. Putting in my get crunk CD, I blasted Big Sean's *I Don't Fuck With You* as I headed out in traffic. Stacks sent me a text letting me know that I was late and everyone was waiting on me to begin. *Perfect*; I thought as I planned on making my grand entrance. I was going to make this nigga see what he was missing out on since he wanted to play games.

Ten minutes later, I was finally pulling into the headquarters. Reaching in my glove compartment, I grabbed my Gucci Guilty perfume and sprayed it all over my body. As I was exiting my car, I could have sworn I saw Joey parked on the other side lurking. I tried to get a better look, but when the person realized that I was walking towards their way, they sped off.

I planned on bringing this to Stacks' attention; I was no longer shrugging shit off. If it ain't feel right then it wasn't right. With the kidnapping of my twins, I learned how to always follow my first gut instinct and since my women's intuition was telling me that Joey was following me then, that was what I was going on. I made a mental not to add more security around my kids.

Chapter 34

Stacks

I sat at the head of the table waiting for Lala to come and join us. I had some important information that I felt like everyone should know. Looking down at my watch, Lala was now almost an hour late. I was about to call her until I heard heels clicking in the hallway.

Lala's perfume arrived and took a seat before she did. When she finally made it to the door, I was at a loss for words. She was rocking the hell out of the Gucci suit. I chuckled a little because I knew what she was up to. She wanted a nigga to see what she was missing.

Little did she know, I was missing her ass every night. It was hard for me to sleep in a lonely ass hotel every night when my family was at home. I had a few cops on my payroll ensuring their safety, but I should have been there with them sleeping on my side of the bed.

"Sorry, I'm late," she said taking a seat at the head of the table that was across from me.

"Now, that fashion show is complete, we can began," I smirked. "Jimmy has some information that he would like to share with us.

Ever since the day Jimmy presented me with the information that he got from working Lala's case when she disappeared, I decided to add him to my payroll. When Ralph started telling me how he didn't trust the dude that Lala was messing with, I had Jimmy check him out for me.

The information that he had was already something that he wanted to share with me. After learning what I did, I was shocked out of my mind. I couldn't believe a pig was so close to my empire.

"Since everybody got moves to make and there's money to be made, I'mma sum it up for you. The nigga that Lala was fucking with is a detective, detective Joey Armstrong to be exact. He is also fucking with Ashley, the same bitch that hired Jimmy to try to take Lala out.

He is also related to Lisa and Jimmy, that's their half brother. Joey and his father, Chief Armstrong was gunning for me. Since I was dead, they decided to go after Lala instead. Now that I'm back, the motherfuckers are back on my ass."

"Damn nigga, so what's the plan?" Ralph asked.

"Sorry to you Lisa and Jimmy but I'mma have to body your brother and father then, we have to switch everything up. I'm not sure how much information he was able to gather, so I want everything switched up. I also want only the lieutenants to know of these changes that way if there's a leak somewhere, I'll be able to plug that shit up immediately."

"I don't care, do what the fuck you want with them pussy ass niggas. His bitch ass wife is the reason our mother is no longer living anyways. If you want me to handle this for you, I'll do it for free," Jimmy suggested.

"Nah kid, you did enough. Good looking out," I said giving him a pound. "But this right here is something that I want to handle on my own." If it was anybody else, I would have allowed Jimmy to handle it, but because it was his brother and father, I decided to do the dirty work on my own. I did not want any slip ups.

"Who was behind the kidnappings of the kids?" Lala asked.

"It was Ashley's ass, but don't worry baby I have something nice planned for their little family. Any more questions?" I asked looking around the room. Everyone shook their head no. "Meeting adjourned. Lala you stay."

I watched as everyone left of out of the conference room leaving Lala and I alone.

"Did you know he was a cop?"

"Hell no, Stacks, if I did I would have never fucked with him like that."

"No puedo creer esto. Mi esposa estaba follando con un cerdo! (I can't believe this. My wife was fucking with a pig!)" I exhaled, rubbing my hands over my waves.

"Si su esposa de sabido que era un cerdo que hubiera sido muerto. (If your wife would of known he was a pig he would have been dead by now.)" she replied shocking the hell out of me. I had no idea she knew how to speak Spanish, this Lala of mines was filled with surprises.

"So, you speaking Spanish now?"

"I picked up a little bit while you was away."

"That shit is sexy as fuck! I said grabbing my dick. "Me encantaría que golpear por la espalda mientras estás hablando a mí en español. (I would love to hit it from the back while you're speaking to me in Spanish.)"

Lala stood up then started to undress. She took off everything leaving the pumps on her feet. She sat on the edge of the conference table with her legs spread wide open. Her pussy was fat and neatly shaved. She had a pretty pussy. Her thighs wasn't discolored and she had no razor bumps.

"Venga conseguirlo papi. (Come get it daddy)," she purred dipping her hands in her pussy causing her wetness to drip down my desk.

"Usted no tiene que decirme dos veces. (You don't have to tell me twice.)" I said kneeling in front of her and then dipping my tongue in her pussy.

"Oooooo Papi," she gasped as I took her clit in my mouth and sucked on it using my tongue to add pressure to it. I hummed on her clit causing a vibration sensation.

Rolling my tongue all around in her wetness, I took each of her pussy lips in my mouth and gently sucked on them. By now, her pussy juices were forming puddles on the desk. I stuck two fingers deep in her fucking her with them while I played hide and go seek with her clit.

I felt her pussy contracting around my fingers, so I pushed them deeper in her and sucked faster on her clit. Her legs started to shake. I held them tightly around my neck and continued to suck until my mouth became saturated with her cum.

Swallowing every drop, I pulled out my dick and sat in my chair. She wasted no time getting off the desk and slobbing down my knob. She filled her mouth with saliva and used is to lubricate my dick before sucking me whole. I was hitting the back of her throat and like a pro she didn't gag.

Every time my dick would get to her throat, she would swallow hard on it causing my dick to jump each time. Sucking me with no mercy, I unloaded my seeds down her throat. She spit the nut on the tip of my dick and allowed it to drip down before sucking it all off causing my dick to twitch from the tingling sensation.

Mounting my dick, she slid down and began bouncing on it. She rotated her hips in a circular motion trying to get the right amount of friction on her clit. I felt her legs began to tremble again, so I lifted her and sat her directly on my face and sucked on her clit until a tsunami of her cum trickled down my face.

"Assume the position," I ordered.

Lala got on the edge of the desk on all fours with her face down and her ass tooted high in the air. Removing my wife beater from underneath my dress shirt, I used it to tie her hands around her back. I was about to beat the pussy up and I didn't need her trying to push away from me.

I slid my dick in her slowly and started to make slow strokes. When her pussy got wet enough, I sped up the process digging deep in her guts.

"Dios mío (OH, MY GOD!)," she yelled out as I began to dig deeper and deeper in her.

"You, God, what?"

"Noooooo."

SMACK! SMACK!

"What you telling me no for?" I groaned smacking her ass while I slammed my dick in and out of her pussy.

"I can't," she cried out.

"You can't what?"

"Take the dick... uh... oh shit I'm about to nut!" she screamed as she climaxed.

"How you can't take the dick and you nutting all over it?" I laughed.

Flipping her on her side, I pushed one of her legs back until it was touching her ears then, rammed my dick right back in her. I was fucking some sense in her head since she wanted to walk around and be hardheaded and shit.

"Slow down," she panted.

"You tapping out so soon?"

"No it's… I… Can't… Oh, mierda voy a matarte! (Oh fuck I am going to kill you.)" she yelled as her pussy creamed all over my dick again.

I untied her hands and placed her on her back. Placing each of her legs in the crook of my arms, I began to beat the pussy up again. This time I felt my nut build up as her wet pussy started to pull me in. My dick was drowning in her wetness waiting for me to save it, but there was nothing I could do.

I tried to hold in my nut so that I could further put a hurting on her pussy, but it was feeling too damn good.

My legs began to buckle and I felt my knees get weak. She fed off my weakness and started fucking me back. Holding on to her hips, I matched her thrust until I let in all go in her.

"You fucked up the desk," I said taking a seat in my chair.

"Whose fault is that?"

"Yours, you told your pussy to be so wet." I watched her ass jiggle as she walked to the bathroom to get us rags to clean up.

"How far are you in planning our wedding," I asked as she wiped my dick off.

"I ain't think you still wanted me to plan the wedding the way you just up and left."

"When my side of my closet is cleared then, you know I really mean business because once I move out all my clothes that mean I have no plans on moving it back in."

"I hear you."

"So, what you not trying to marry a nigga?"

"I didn't say that."

"Then get to planning," I said smacking her on the ass. "I'll be home later on tonight and a nigga feel like eating a steak."

***

Ralph and I sat in front of Chief Armstrong's house staking the place out. Jimmy told me how Joey thought so highly of his father, so I decided to kill his ass first, make him suffer the loss of his father then, take him out of his misery. Jimmy requested that I leave the mother untouched. He wanted to be the one to avenge the death of his mother and I agreed as long as she stayed out of our way.

A little after midnight, the chief came home, but with a white younger woman that I am sure wasn't his wife. It was one thing to cheat on your wife, but to bring the hoe back to the home you shared with her was just dumb as fuck. We waited for them to get deep inside before going in the house.

Ralph was able to pick the locks with no problems. This dude really thought he was untouchable because he didn't even have a security system in his house. Once we were inside, we heard moaning coming from the bedroom. *He could at least fuck the thot in the bathroom*; I thought as I watched his little dick ass get sucked on by the snow bunny. She had a funny look on her face and he looked as if he was all into it. She was probably a hooker that got busted and was now paying off her debt, so she wouldn't go to jail.

Screwing on my silencer, I aimed my gun to his head and shot twice splitting it open. Before the girl could react, Ralph shot her in the head dropping her on the floor. Going to the car, I pulled out the dead pig I was able to buy in a rotisserie in Spanish town. I placed the dead pig next to his dead body. With a black marker I wrote on the wall,

ALL PIGS MUST DIE!

Making sure everyone was dead; we left as quietly as we came in. Getting in the car, we removed the plastic suits that we wore over our clothes to prevent any of our DNA from getting in the house. I pulled out a black bag and we placed the suits, gloves, and hairnets in it. I drove to a nearby dumpster and burned all the evidence. Driving to Little Haiti, we took the guns we used in the murders to a Zoe Pound nigga that I paid good money to get rid of them. I then drove the little Honda I used in the murder to a closed field where I set it on fire. We walked to the IHOP and waited for Lisa to come pick us up.

It was a little after two a.m. when I got home and a nigga was hungry as fuck. When I walked in the house, I walked to the kitchen in search for something to eat. Lala left a note on the refrigerator telling me that my food was in the oven. I heated it up in the microwave then grabbed the sour cream for my bake potato. Taking a bite of the steak, it was well done and well seasoned just the way I liked it. I finished my first plate and went to go heat up some seconds.

"Your greedy ass," Lala said standing the doorway.

"Oh, shit I was about to blast your ass for scaring a nigga like that."

"I just sat and watch you eat two plates of food," she laughed and grabbed a bottle of water.

"I gotta eat in order to keep giving you that good dick," I said taking a bite of my potato.

"Whatever, I'm going to bed."

"I want you on that bed naked and waiting for me," I said as she walked out of the kitchen.

Cleaning off my plate, I placed it in the dishwasher and went to go check on my kids. I kissed both of them on the cheeks as they lay in their bed sleeping peacefully. I said a silent prayer of protection over them before walking out of their room. I went to the bathroom and quickly brushed my teeth. Just as I requested, Lala was in bed naked waiting for me.

Chapter 35

Joey

Looking at the crime scene photos in my father's murder enraged me. Although there was no evidence to prove it, I was one hundred percent positive that Stacks had something to do with my father's death.

There was also another woman that wasn't my mother that was found dead on the scene as well. To protect my father's name, I made sure that nothing was said to the press about the mysterious woman that my father was cheating on my mother with.

I haven't slept for three days. I was busy trying to find something to connect Stacks to the murder of my father, but I kept coming up short. He was a clever little fucker, but I was going to bring his ass down. I reached out to both Lisa and Jimmy and invited them to our father's funeral, but the basically told me that they could careless if he was dead or alive. My mother was in no condition to make funeral arrangements, so I took it upon myself to make them for her.

When my father's insurance policies kicked in, I planned on moving my mother out of Miami. I didn't want to risk Stacks getting to her. I had already made plans to move her, Ashley, and the kids to South Carolina to live with my aunt until Stacks and every motherfucker associated with him was either dead or behind bars.

Even though I didn't have a way to get to him now, I planned on raiding all of his traps and putting as many of his workers in jail as possible. Eventually one of them would be facing serious charges and I'll be able to cut a deal with them in exchange for information on Stacks.

The morning of my father's funeral was very gloomy. The sky was grey as light raindrops dripped onto the ground. I rode in the limo in silence as memories of my father began to flood my mind. Even though he was hard on me I knew deep inside he only did it because he saw I had so much potential in me. He wanted me to fill his shoes and even though he was gone, I vowed to make him proud of me.

The church was beautifully decorated as everyone sat in attendance. The whole police department was there dressed in their uniform in honor of my father. The mayor was even there sitting in the back of the church. My father was so well respected and everyone loved him. Walking to the front of the pew, I took a seat in the first row that was designated for family members. I sat in the middle of my mother and Ashley offering them both comfort.

A slide show of my father and the years he worked was presented. At the end of the show there wasn't a dry eye in the church. The mayor stood in front of the church and presented me with awards that my father had earned and I gratefully accepted them on his behalf. When it came time for me to speak, my mouth became dry and the words wouldn't form. I stood in the front of the church and just broke out crying. There was a lot that I could say about my father but nothing was going to bring him back.

We headed to the gravesite to say our final goodbyes. An American flag decorated the top of my father's casket as the police officers shot their riffles in attempt to say their last goodbyes. Before my father's casket was lowered into the ground, two officers neatly folded the American flag and presented it to my mother along with a plaque of recognition.

Everyone was leaving and getting into their cars when a swarm of all black Escalades with dark tinted windows started shooting up the funeral. The parking lot was chaotic as everyone ran trying to avoid getting hit by a stray bullet. I ran for my son picking him up and then ran towards Ashley and handed him to her.

"Stay right here and don't move," I yelled out pulling out my gun and shooting back. The officers immediately pulled out their guns and started shooting at the cars, but with all of us we still were no match for the type of ammunition they had.

I watched as a few officers' bodies began to fall to the ground one by one like a domino affect. The way they was shooting you would have thought it was fireworks on the forth of Jul. Finally surrendering, I took cover behind a car and waited for the shooting to stop. The sounds of screeching tires could be heard as they pulled off.

It was a blood bath at my father's funeral as bodies of officers and innocent bystanders decorated the parking lot floor. I was walking towards the ambulance to see how many of my officers were done until I saw the coroner covering my mother's body with a black sheet.

"Noooooo," I cried as I ran towards her, but it was too late; she was already dead. I sat there on the ground with her lifeless body in my arms praying to God for this to just be a nightmare. I just buried my father, and would to have to bury my mother too. It all broke my heart. I was now a motherless child. The only parent I had left was snatched from me by Stacks and today was the day I was going to take everyone he loved away from him.

I grabbed Ashley hand as we left the crime scene and headed home. I needed to hurry up and get them packed and out of Miami before Stacks took away the only two people I had left. Lala knew about my daughter, I wasn't too worried because I never told her that she was away in England attending boarding school.

"How long do we have to leave for?" Ashley asked.

"For as long as it takes me to handle this situation."

"If you would have just been honest with me we could have worked together."

"Ashley, not now. I don't have time for your shit. I just want to get you and my son out of here so that I can handle my business."

"Whatever," she said rolling her eyes. I wanted to so badly knock them out of her head, but I had to remember that my son was in the car with us.

"Only pack a light bag of things you and my son will need. I will send you money to get everything else you need," I said as we pulled up in front of the house.

I grabbed my son out of his car seat and stuck my key in the door opening it. I made sure Ashley was inside before closing and locking the door behind me. As soon as the lock on the door clicked, the house exploded. The impact of the explosion caused me to fly to the back of the room.

My head hit the corner of the glass table real hard before I hit the ground. I tried my best to keep my eyes open, but I was losing too much blood from the deep gash that I had on my head.

Looking across the room, I could see that Ashley's body had hit the wall causing the heavy bookcase to fall on top of her. I tried to call out to her, but it was as if my voice box was snatched out of my throat. I looked at her and prayed for her to move, but she never did.

Mustering all of my energy I crawled over to my son who was softly whimpering. He wasn't really hurt too bad because I was holding him causing his fall not to do a lot of damage to his little body.

The house was covered in flames as I tried to find a way to escape. There was no way I was going to get out of the house with Ashley and the baby in my condition. I tried to reach for my phone, but I became really light headed. I was starting to lose too much blood. I attempted again to grab my phone and this time I was successful. I dialed 911 then waited for the operator.

"911, what 's you emergency."

"This is detective Joey Armstrong and my house is in flames," I managed to say before everything went black.

Chapter 36
Lisa

Sitting at my parents' gravesite with a bottle of Patron, balloons, and teddy bears, today was a day of celebration. I was celebrating finally being able to avenge their deaths. At first, I just thought they died in a car crash, but when I found out that Joey's bitch ass mama was the one to take them away from me because she wanted to be a bitter bitch, I was out for blood.

Jimmy and I came up with a plan to shoot up that bitch ass nigga funeral and to kill his wife. As badly as I wanted to kill Joey and Ashley ass, I had to let them live. Stacks wanted to be the one to end it for them and I couldn't help but respect it. Putting the bullets in that bitch's head gave me the same rush I felt when I killed Tasha's bitch ass. I guess being a killer was in my blood after all.

"Bae you ready to go?" Ralph asked walking up to me.

"Yes, give me a minute. I'll meet you in the car." I waited until he was gone before speaking to my parents.

"Mommy and daddy, I love both you dearly and I hope now with them motherfuckers dead you guys can now rest in peace. Hold my spot down for me," I said kissing both of their tombstones then, pouring the bottle of liquor on the ground.

I felt something that I haven't felt in a while as I walked through the graveyard, and that was happiness. My life was finally starting to get back on track. I was understanding my worth and figuring out my purpose. I had the love of my life with me, my best friend by my side, and it felt good.

"Where are we going?" I asked Ralph as I noticed that we wasn't heading in the direction towards any of our houses.

"Just chill I have surprise for you."

"You know I don't like surprise."

"I do, but you'll love this one trust me.'

"Who house is this?" I asked as we pulled up to a two story family house.

"Shut up and get out of the car. You ask too many questions."

We got out of the car and I watched him take out a set of keys that had a bow around them and handed them to me.

"Would like to do the honors?" he asked.

When what he was saying finally registered in my head, I jumped in his arms kissing him all over the face.

"Oh, my God, is this my house?" I asked.

"It's OUR house," he replied putting me down so that I could open the door.

The house was empty except for a neatly dressed table that was in the middle of the family room. The house was dimly lit and there was a waiter standing there next to the table holding a bottle of champagne.

Ralph pulled out a chair for me and I took a seat. I was at a loss for words because no guy had really done anything this nice for me. Ralph and I made small talk about our new house as we sat and ate a meal that consisted of shrimp, crab, and lobster pasta, baked tilapia, mash potatoes, asparagus, and freshly baked cheddar biscuits.

"You ready for desert," Ralph asked as the waiter began to clear the table.

"I don't think I can eat no more. I am stuffed."

"C'mon now, I heard this is the best strawberry cheese cake in town you gotta eat some."

"Ok, but in the morning, I'm waking up extra early to run this off."

"You tripping. I love my woman with a little extra meat on them."

The waiter came back in the room and sat five small containers in front of me.

"I hope you don't expect me to eat all of this?"

"Just open them."

I opened the first one and it was a small cake that read **WILL** the second one read **YOU** opening the third one tears began to flood my eyes as I read the word **Marry**.

"Yes!!!!" I shouted before I could open the rest of the containers.

"You have to open the rest of them," he laughed.

Cooperating I opened the last of the containers, the fourth one had the word **ME?** and the fifth one had a gorgeous princess cut pink and black diamond engagement ring. My mouth dropped to the ground as the diamonds in the ring shimmered so beautifully.

"So, we doing this or nah?" he asked on one knee.

"Yes!" I screamed out as he placed the ring on my finger. Thank God Lala talked me into getting a manicure because I would have been mad if I had to wear this beautiful ring with my finger looking all knocked up. I took a picture of the ring on my finger and sent it to Lala with the message *I said yes!*

"You just made me the happiest man alive."

"No, you just made me the happiest woman alive."

"You ready to bless our new house," he asked lifting me up in his arms

"Yes bae!"

The house wasn't furnished yet so Ralph had a nice little pallet made on the floor for us. He laid me down on it and began ripping my clothes off. He then buried his head deep in my pussy and started making it love to it.

I tried to move his head deeper between my legs, but he pinned both of my arms over my head holding it there. He ate me out with so much passion that when I finally came, I had tears in my eyes.

"Damn the tongue got your ass crying and shit," he joked finally coming up for air.

"Shut up, I'm crying because I'm happy."

"Aww, look at my lil thug getting all soft on me and shit."

"You gon' give me the dick or are you going to sit up here and talk shit?"

"Both," he said as he entered me.

My phone started to ring and by the sound of the ringtone, I could tell that it was Lala. She was going to have to wait until the morning. I had plans on fucking my fiancé in every inch of our new house.

Chapter 37

Unknown Female

Today was the day of Lala and Stacks' wedding and I'll be damned if I was going to allow them to have their happily every after. I sat in the chair as the personal stylist that I hired for this special event beat my face to the Gods. Examining my face in the mirror, I was on point.

My eyebrows were on fleek and arched to perfection, my hair was laid, and my face was just amazing. Thanking my stylist, I gave her a two hundred dollar tip and told her to let herself out as I went upstairs to get dressed.

Dressed in a black and white crossover bandaged dress, I left little to the imagination. I made sure the dress was tight enough to revel the small baby bump I was sporting. Spraying myself with my Daisy perfume I slipped my feet in a pair of black Dolce and Gabbana pumps. I turned around in my full body mirror making sure that everything was in place. Grabbing my pink MAC lip-gloss I made sure my lips were extra glossy.

The wedding was being held on the beach and the reception on their yacht. I had to give it to Lala she really did have great taste. I followed her around for months as her and her wedding planner planned her wedding I was low key jealous, but after tonight I was sure Stacks would finally be mine for good.

Since today was a day filled with festivities, I decided to drive my cocaine white Audi convertible. When I arrived to the weeding, I made sure to place my oversized Dolce and Gabbana shades over my face. I didn't want anyone to recognize me until it was my time to reveal myself. I sat in the very back and waited for the wedding that I was about to crash to begin.

Chapter 38

Stacks

I sat in my dresser room checking myself out in the all white Armani suit I was wearing. My face was neatly shaved, my haircut was on point, a nigga was looking and feeling good. Today was the day I was taking myself off the market for good and I had no problems with doing that.

Lala was the love of my life, the mother of my children, and although we'd been through hell and back we always found our way back together. She was my soul mate and there was no way I was going to live my life without her being apart of it.

The wedding cost me eighty grand and it was worth all my hard earned money. Just to see the smile on my wife face as she put her all into planning this event was priceless. I would have been ok with us getting married in the courthouse, but she wanted something small and intimate, so I was cool with it. A soft knock at my door interrupted me from my thoughts. Getting up to open the door, I was greeted by my twins they were now eleven months old and walking and running around.

"Da-da," my baby girl called out to my opening her arms, so that I could pick her up. She looked so cute in her white little dress with her yellow bows neatly tying up her head filled with curls. Kissing her on the cheeks, I put her down and picked up my handsome son that was looking sharper than ever in his mini all white Armani suit. Next month, my kids would be one, so it was time for me to put another baby in Lala. If I was lucky another set of twins.

"Bruh, you ready?" Ralph asked taking a seat on the red plush sofa that was in my dressing room.

"I don't think I am going to be more ready than this."

"My dawg about to be off the thot market," he laughed.

"I been off the thot market bruh and what you laughing for? You next."

"Yeah, I hear you. Ain't shit out there but hoodrats and bitches with their hands out. We got us some good women."

"Five minutes." The planner knocked on the door interrupting our conversation "I was looking everywhere for you babies," she said picking up the twins and walking out the room with them

"I hear you bruh. Let's get this show on the road." I said grabbing my suit jacket and putting it on.

Taking my spot under the shed that Lala and I were going to get married under, I took a look at our guest. We didn't fuck with too many people so there were only about sixty people in attendance. The wedding started as Ralph and Lisa walked down the aisle pulling the twins in a wagon. When they took their place, I waked up to the mic and waited for the instrumental to play. Lala had no clue that she would to be walking down the aisle to my voice. I had the wedding planner to keep that part a secret.

Ooh, ooh hoo, I wanna be, girl, let me be
I wanna be everything your man's not
And I'm gonna give you every little thing I've got
'Cause you are more than a man needs
That's why I say you're truly my destiny

I'm gonna getcha if it takes me until forever
No, you don't feel me, if forever turns into never
I'll let you know my love is just as strong
And for you never just ain't that long, ohh

I wanna be the smile you put on your face
(Oh, yes)
I wanna be your hands when you say your grace
(Say it, baby)
I wanna be whatever is your favorite place
(Girl)
Oh, I just wanna be close

(Close to you)

I began to sing the words to Avant I *Wanna Be Close* as Lala walked down the aisle wearing a beautiful custom made all white Vera Wang dress that she had custom made. She looked breathtaking as she walked down the aisle with the assistance of my father. The closer she got, I noticed that she had tears coming out of her eyes. It was getting real hard for me to sing the song without choking up.

See my life's filled with up and downs
(My life's filled)
(Up and downs)
I'm okay when you're around
(I'm okay)
(Yeah)
And when I'm in a storm and my nights are cold
(In a storm)
Reach out your hands for me to hold
(Out your hands)
(For me to hold)

See you're my queen on a throne

(My queen)

(Yeah)

And you're the reason for a song

(This song)

And I can't wait

(Can't wait)

To fill you up with love

(Fill you up with love)

Fill you with love

I wanna be the sun your stars and your moon

I wanna be a hot summer day in June

I wanna be the smell of your sweet perfume

I just wanna be close

I was able to finish up the song without shedding a tear. When my father gave Lala away to me then, I lost it. I wasn't able to hold back the tears. Embracing my soon to be wife, I held her tight in my arms as my tears stained her dress. No matter how much of a thug you were, every nigga was bound to cry on their wedding day. Just seeing the love of your life so beautiful knowing that you're about to stand before God and make that woman yours forever was a very emotional thing. Getting myself together, I used the back of my hand to wipe my tears and the pastor to begin.

"Anthony Stacks Jones." Lala laughed as she began her vows. "The love of my life. The man that saved me from a horrible relationship and showed me what it felt like to truly feel loved. I still remember the day I crashed in the back of your car. I still can feel those same butterflies that I felt when I first laid eyes on you. Once upon a time, I thought that James was the love of my life. I thought it would be him standing here in your spot and it was us getting married. But God has a funny way of working. What you want isn't always what you need. God put you in my life not only to be my husband, but to be my best friend, my partner. For us to become one. We now have three beautiful children and I can only wish that God continues to bless our family. I love you with all my heart and I am truly honored to become Mrs. Anthony Jones."

"Three kids? Are you pregnant?" I asked looking her in the eyes that were now clouded with tears. She nodded her head yes and the crowd began to clap and cheer.

"Lala Williams, my queen. I am at loss for words right now; you caught me off guard with that one. I'm usually on top of my game with finding out before you do, but I guess you caught me slipping." I laughed. "I'm just so ready to spend the rest of my life with you. I am ready to show you how it feels to be treated like royalty I am ready to wake up to you every morning as husband and wife. I'm ready to come home to a house filled with babies. I love everything about you from your smile to the way you snore. I believe that we were meant for one another and I am the luckiest man alive to have a wonderful woman as yourself to call my wife."

"Do anyone here know why these two shouldn't be married? Speak now." the pastor spoke out to the crowd.

"I do," I heard a voice said and I pulled out my gun and turned around and pointed toward the person's directions.

As she removed the big hat and the shades that she was wearing, I instantly froze. I was at a loss for words as my past decided to come fuck with me on my wedding day.

"Those two shouldn't be married because I am also pregnant with Stacks' child," she said as she rubbed her hand over her small baby bump "I guess you're about to be a father of Four," she laughed

Lala snatched the gun out of my hand and pointed it in her direction.

"Lala noooo!!" I yelled trying to reach for the gun. No matter how bad I wanted to body the bitch, I had to make sure that the baby she was carrying was mine first. There was a chance that I could have fathered her baby and if in fact that was my child, I would feel like shit if something was to happen to it.

Lala's eyes was filled with so much pain and hurt as she pointed the gun directly at the wedding crasher's stomach. Her fingers began inching towards the trigger, so I tackled her to the ground trying to get the gun from her, but it was too late.

POW! POW! POW!

TO BE CONTINUED…...

CPSIA information can be obtained
at www.ICGtesting.com
Printed in the USA
LVOW02s0020070617
537193LV00009B/114/P